ABOUT THIS BOOK

A coven of witches in suburbia, juggling families and holidays and jealousy, or fighting with the local homeowners' association with both magic and their wits.

Magic users in Portland, OR, who have a special and unusual relationship with their familiars.

This collection contains three stories from the fan-favorite Desperate Housewitches series and the popular Portland Hedge-witches series.

So brew up some potion, settle in with your cat, and lose yourself in these stories of glamour and occasional infighting from a master of urban fantasy!

"Trust Dayle to write a winter holiday story about the solstice and magic. She manages to combine the claustrophobia of a suburban neighborhood with the competitiveness that women sometimes engage in with holiday ritual. Only the holiday ritual here isn't decorating a Christmas tree or singing carols (although there is a discussion of carolers that made me chuckle). Nope. This one is about pagan rituals. [Desperate Housewitches is] wonderful, funny, and a do-not-miss."

—Kristine Kathryn Rusch
Hugo-award winning author

Desperate Housewitching
Dayle A. Dermatis

Print edition published 2024 by Soul's Road Press

ISBN 978-1-946462-27-5

"Desperate Housewitches" originally appeared in *Uncollected Anthology* Issue 2: *Winter Witches*, 2014.
"The Real Housewitches of Calafia County" originally appeared in *WMG Holiday Spectacular*, 2019.
"A Witch in Time" originally appeared in *Cutter's Final Cut*, Issue 4: *Witches*, 2022.
"Hedging the Witch" originally appeared in *Uncollected Anthology*, Issue 10: *Fabulous Familiars*.
"Releasing the Spell" originally appeared in *Uncollected Anthology*, Issue 12: *Spells Gone Awry*.
"Telling the Bees" originally appeared in *Uncollected Anthology*, Issue 18: *Beasties*.

Inquiries should be addressed to
Soul's Road Press
info@soulsroadpress.com
http://www.soulsroadpress.com

Cover image © linaflerova | Depositphotos
Soul's Road Press logo: Designs by Trapdoor

DESPERATE HOUSEWITCHING

TALES OF URBAN MAGIC

DAYLE A. DERMATIS

SOUL'S ROAD PRESS

THE DESPERATE HOUSEWITCHES SERIES

DESPERATE HOUSEWITCHES

DESPERATE
HOUSEWITCHES
Don't mess with *this* coven!
DAYLE A.
DERMATIS
"…One of the best writers working today."
– USA Today bestselling author Dean Wesley Smith

ABOUT THIS STORY

Kim reigns as the witchy Martha Stewart of her neighborhood coven...until Philippa moves in across the street, with her snooty English pagan heritage and her magical one-upmanship.

When the annual Winter Solstice ritual goes horribly wrong, can Kim and Philippa put their differences aside and bring back the sun?

A funny, pointed story about holiday rituals from a master of urban fantasy!

DESPERATE HOUSEWITCHES

It started with the Samhain decorations.

It would get worse at Yule.

Much worse.

I just didn't know that yet.

"I just don't like her," I said between gritted teeth, furiously polishing a silver quaich, the shallow bowl with two stag's heads as handles that we needed for our Samhain ritual.

"Jealousy is a negative emotion, and it'll suck away your energy if you let it continue," Dana said reasonably.

Dana was my best friend; we'd grown up in this neighborhood together, taken over our respective mothers' places in the coven when it came time, brought in husbands and, in her case, started raising children. She was small and slender and looked like most people's idea of a fairy, with blond ringlets and impossibly wide blue eyes—an image that was shattered whenever she cursed, because she had a hell of a potty mouth.

She was my best friend and I loved her, even when she was right and I stubbornly refused to admit it.

We were in my house, a Gothic Victorian with a widow's walk (unnecessary in a neighborhood not remotely near the ocean, but still charming) and stained glass framing the windows. All the houses on our block are different styles, from Painted Ladies to Craftsman bungalows. There's even a black-beamed, white-stuccoed Tudor the next street over. Some people say our houses slowly conform to the owners.

They wouldn't be wrong.

The kitchen smelled like pumpkin and spices, which made sense, because I was baking for the ritual as well. Of course we'd have the traditional cakes and ale as part of the ceremony, but I also always made extra to send home with everyone.

"I'm *not* jealous," I said.

Dana pointed out the window, across the street to Philippa's house (Arts and Crafts Movement, and I happen to know it looked like William Morris had exploded inside). "You're telling me that you don't feel threatened that she's probably going to win Best Decorated House this year?"

Of *course* I felt threatened. I'd won Best Decorated House for the past ten years, ever since I set up residence here. In our coven, I was the one with the best decorations, the best food at potlucks, the best parties, the best poison garden (for show only, of course)…it was my *thing*. Everybody knew it was my thing, and everybody loved me for it.

And then Philippa had come to town. Pretty Philippa, with her stupid English accent and her high-and-mighty "I'm from England so I know how the rituals are really supposed to go" and her Goddess-damned *decorations*.

I put down the quaich and picked up the chalice of simple beaten silver. Before I attacked it with the polishing cloth, though, I closed my eyes and took a deep, cleansing breath. In through the nose, out through the mouth. Ground, center. If I let my negative energy seep into the tools, the Solstice ritual would go all wonky, and you did *not* want anything to go wrong at Samhain, when the Veil Between the Worlds was thinnest. No telling what might come through.

I could have used magic to polish the ritual tools—just like I could've used magic to keep my house clean and tidy, bake all the holiday goodies, grow my herbs and vegetables. (Okay, sometimes I encouraged the plants—but I still got my hands in the dirt and pulled all the weeds.) But that would be missing the point. Everything in life was Ritual, and you imbued your personal magic in it *as* you did the work. You didn't use magic *instead* of doing the work.

The meditation helped; I felt centered in what I was doing, knowing it was right. But as I commenced polishing, I couldn't help glancing out the window again, and I felt my blood pressure start to creep up again.

Philippa used magic for everything.

The maple trees outside Philippa's house seemed to be producing the brightest flaming leaves on the block—and even the leaves on the ground didn't seem to be losing their color, arranging themselves artfully, as if in a painting titled something twee like "Enchanted Autumn" or "Tree of Fire."

Ravens—real ones. How she convinced those ornery buggers to stick around, I don't know, and I wasn't about to admit they really added a certain something. Garlands of black oak leaves and a vase of black roses on the porch (possibly not real, but I wouldn't put it past her). Clusters of impossibly intricately carved jack o'lanterns. Purple and orange lights highlighted every window, every eave, lit and visible even during the day.

Meanwhile, just yesterday, she'd left baskets on everybody's porches, filled with homemade foods of the season: mulled wine and cider, tarts of pumpkin and apple, a thick, hearty stew and fresh bread. That was my *thing*, too, and Philippa had beaten me by one day. *One freaking day*. The gingerbread had been cooling on wire racks when Philippa had dropped off her basket.

She'd included aprons in each of our colors in the baskets. Last year, I'd delivered hand-embroidered dish towels. I figured I still won there.

I also had made adorable witch's hat fascinators to give out at the potluck, so there.

"Nobody loves you any less," Dana said. "Maybe it's okay for you to step back and let someone else have a little of the limelight. Maybe you can *relax* and not feel so much pressure to be perfect."

"I don't feel any pressure to be perfect," I protested, and I really didn't. "I *like* doing all this. And I like things just so. I like things organized and familiar." I knew I sounded just a skosh whiny when I added, "Philippa's messing everything up."

"She wouldn't've been able to move here if she didn't fit in with our core beliefs," Dana, ever logical, pointed out. "We all agreed."

"I didn't say she was a bad person, or a bad pagan," I said. "I said she was pissing me off."

Dana went to the oven and pulled out the pies about two seconds before the timer went off, because she had a bit of pre-cog ability.

"And I don't blame you for that," she said, her cheeks flushing from the heat. "But it seems like she's here to stay, and you're going to have to find a way to coexist with her."

I did the mental equivalent of sticking my fingers in my ears and chanting "I can't hear you."

Because for all our skill at divination, no witch can see the specifics of the future. (Remember, kids, prophecies are open to interpretation, and you're likely to pick the wrong one. So just don't go there.)

～

Philippa beat my hat fascinators with seasonal incense, specifically magicked for each of the thirteen of us. *And* she won Best Decorated House.

The ritual was a little strained, but nothing untowards happened.

It was uncharitable of me, and I knew it, but I still seethed. And plotted how to outdo her—outdo myself—at the Winter Solstice.

～

It started, again, with decorations.

Philippa snuck hers up in the middle of the night, it seemed, because December first dawned on evergreens (yes, she *changed what kinds of trees she had in her front yard*) draped in ropes of glowing snowflakes, and her house had garlands of holly and ivy, and huge lit-up holly and oak leaves in the wide front window. Holiday music emanated from her yard at all hours of the day and night—not loud or obnoxious, but the white lights that adorned her house and the trees blinked and shimmered with the beat.

Did I mention the smells? Pine and nutmeg and peppermint; you caught whiffs as you walked by. Not all at once, of course.

Then there was the horse. Philippa had told us all, more than once (ad nauseum), that her name meant "lover of horses" and that the horse was her spirit animal. So she'd put out a life-sized Hooden Horse with its companions: a groom with a whip, several musicians, and a man dressed in women's clothing. (The British seem to be big on the latter, if their holiday pantomimes are anything to go by.)

"From East Kent, apparently, but you see similar traditions in Caerleon, Wales, and Lancashire," Dana told me. She and I and our friend Maggie were in Dana's plant-filled sunroom—which felt sunny even though the glowering sky threatened more snow—drinking tea spiced with cloves and cinnamon and orange, and wrapping presents. I'd made cloth bags out of all my appropriate scrap fabric for the year, and was sorting bags to gifts based on size, and estimating how much cord I'd need to weave.

I paused to look at Dana, raising an eyebrow. I didn't even have to say anything.

"She told me about it when she had me over for coffee," Dana said. My eyebrow didn't waver. "I can visit her for coffee without betraying our friendship," Dana protested.

I didn't ask her whose house decorations she'd voted for at Samhain. I didn't want to know.

And yes, she was right: she could visit whomever she darn well wanted.

The Hooden Horse's wooden head was festooned with bells and rosettes. Its jaw was hinged, and it would crack shut at various intervals. According to my own research, the head on a pole was traditionally carried around the big houses of the parish just before Christmas.

What*ever*.

I'd gone with more familiar, traditional decorations, with lights shaped like pentagrams (what, you never noticed that people hang five-pointed stars at the holidays?), big pots of poinsettias (spelled to not be poisonous to neighborhood critters), and life-sized models of the Oak King and the Holly King battling it out on the roof.

How is that not traditional? The Winter Solstice is the longest night of the year, a time when the two Gods (or two aspects of the same God, depending on who you follow) duke it out. The winter Holly King dies to give the next half of the year over to the summer Oak King, which allows the days to start growing longer again. At the Summer Solstice, they'd repeat their fight, and the Holly King would reign again.

Anyway, it was funny that I never saw Philippa put up those middle-of-the-night decorations, given that I had been creeping around the neighborhood at the very same time, hanging mistletoe on everyone's porches.

Yes, I used a little magic so I didn't leave footprints in the snow. So sue me.

"Everyone has different strengths and weaknesses," Maggie said. Her hair had gone pure white when she was in her twenties, and between that and her willowy height and green eyes, she was incredibly striking. She was principal at the local grade school, where she put the fear of the Goddess in all the little children.

"And my weakness is competitiveness; I get it," I said.

"No," Maggie said. "It's not a weakness. You two have to find a way to get along, sure, but it takes two to Tarot, as they say. Philippa should be willing to meet you halfway. She can't just swan in here and expect to change things."

"That's not the point," Dana began, and then her head went up, and I knew her precog ability was acting up because she always looked like a dog with pricked-up ears (in a good way).

I didn't have to be precog to know exactly what was happening when the doorbell rang.

Philippa brought sugar cookies in the shapes of pentacles, and holly and ivy and oak leaves, evergreens, and suns and moons. Of course. She swept into the room, a big smile on her face.

"Dana, Maggie!" She saw me. Her smile faltered, although she gamely tried to paste it back on. "...oh, hello, Kimberly."

Philippa had deep blue eyes and tousled dark hair, into which she'd tucked the fascinator I'd made at Samhain, much to my surprise. It was in her color, midnight blue, with a little scrap of a veil. She had that English peaches-and-cream complexion, and cheekbones that could slice glass. She wore a flowing black lace top, skinny jeans, and lace-up pointed-toe black Victorian boots. A little Helena Bonham Carter, a little Nigella Lawson.

I really hoped that low growl in the back of my throat was something I was just imagining. To be safe, I cleared my throat. "Hi, Philippa. It's good to see you." I even smiled.

Look, even I knew I was acting like an ass. I couldn't change the way I felt, but I had control over what I did despite my feelings. Maggie was probably right: we needed to meet halfway. So I stood, hugged Philippa hello. She smelled like violets, sweet and green, an unexpected scent in the darkening days of winter.

We re-seated ourselves.

"Did you bring any presents to wrap?" Dana asked Philippa.

"Oh, I'm afraid not," Philippa said, and I felt an unGoddess-like twinge of satisfaction before she added, "I've been making paper for two days, and it's not quite ready for wrapping yet."

"You're making your own wrapping paper?" Maggie said. "Wow! Maybe you can do a demo at the school after the holidays."

Hey. I thought Maggie was on *my* side.

Next year, clearly, I was going to have to weave my own cloth to make gift bags.

"Before I forget," I said, even though I hadn't forgotten, but I wanted to make my change of subject seem natural, "has everyone decided what they're bringing to the dessert exchange?"

One of our holiday traditions was a party where everyone brought cookies and other holiday desserts—individual mince pies, pecan squares, brownies, that sort of thing. We sampled and drank wassail and eggnog, and at the end of the evening, everyone went home with an assortment of desserts.

"You're doing your peppermint fudge again, right?" Dana asked.

I shook my head. I had to go for *spectacular* this year. I was thinking about peppermint ice cream bonbons that stayed frozen on their own. I didn't tell them because I wanted it to be a surprise. "I'm branching out."

"Nooooo!" Maggie said. "I love your fudge. It's the best part of Yule!"

"My kids will slay me if I don't come home with it," Dana agreed. "And Georgine is probably going to faint dead away." Our friend Georgine *was* rather dramatic, it was true.

"You will all survive," I said, secretly pleased. Handed down through generations of my family, my peppermint fudge had a secret ingredient that added both taste and magic.

"Hmm…" said Philippa. "I don't suppose there's a list of what everyone's bringing, so we don't all bring the same thing."

"Afraid not," I said, catching myself before I said something about how we all knew because we'd been doing this for years. It really wasn't her fault she was new. It was just her attitude. I could see those wheels turning.

"I think these cookies are wonderful," Dana said, waving one of the pentacle sugar cookies. "Or you could bring something that's been your tradition in the past. Even if it's similar to someone else's, you'll have put your own spin on it."

I actually felt calmer than I had in awhile. My dessert would be the most impressive, I'd get my reputation back, and Philippa would learn to meet me halfway.

It was the perfect plan.

If only I'd had Dana's precog abilities…

~

The annual Solstice dessert exchange was held at my house, largely because my great-grandmother had started the tradition in the neighborhood.

The dark wood paneled wainscoting gleamed under the glow of candles, which I had magically hung in midair above our heads, not close enough to the high ceiling to scorch. (What can I say? I was inspired by *Harry Potter*.) Evergreen garland wove between the white candles in a Celtic knot-work pattern and cast a pine scent throughout the house.

This was my favorite time of year—not the Solstice per se, but the gathering of families. My fellow witch-sisters, their partners, their children and parents. I had differently decorated trees set up in various rooms (one pagan, one colorful, one white and silver and purple, one random child-hood decorations), a full bar as well as wassail warming of its own accord, and games for the children in the playroom. Oh, and the Playstation in the media room for the older kids and the young at heart.

The heavy dining room table of black walnut was covered with my great-grandmother's linen tablecloth and antique tiered serving platters, on which I'd placed white china plates with a delicate holly border and gilded edges. As attendees arrived, they arranged their desserts on the plates. In the kitchen, for later, I had holiday Tupperware for the exchange, decorated with each family's name in calligraphy.

Philippa and her husband, Cecil, arrived. He was blond to her dark, with a solid sort of Rex Harrison thing going on. She was in red, which highlighted her coloring, and she seemed...sort of excited, which was outside of her usual realm of cool and reservedly British.

A moment before I saw Philippa's dessert offering, Dana

was suddenly at my side, Maggie a moment behind her. Uh oh. What had Dana *seen*?

And then I saw what Philippa had brought for the exchange.

Peppermint fudge.

Sweet chocolate and spicy peppermint wafted into my senses, followed by…no. It couldn't be.

Calling energy up from the earth and down from the moon, I squinted at the squares, so prettily decorated with shavings of red, green, and white peppermint flakes, but my sight went past that, into the fudge, into the very ingredients and their proportions. (I told you it was my thing.)

And then I saw it, oh yes I did.

The secret ingredient. Just a hint of candied ginger, which in our tradition speaks of heat, added to keep the eater warm while the sun returns.

My head snapped up. "You stole my recipe?"

Everyone stopped talking. The room got very, very quiet, except for Blackmore's Night's "Mid Winter's Night" singing through the hidden speakers my husband, Eric, had installed.

Philippa's eyes grew larger, if such a thing were even possible. "No, I…I borrowed it. Everyone was saying how much they'd miss your fudge because you weren't making it, so I thought… I didn't think you'd mind…"

"That was a secret recipe handed down through my family," I said. "Guarded, prized. And you…"

Philippa shook her head, color blooming in her pale cheeks. "I had no idea," she whispered. "I just thought people would enjoy it."

Everyone was watching us. I tamped back my anger. Even the question of *how* was suddenly obvious to me. I'd hosted the Solstice ritual planning meeting a few days ago, all thirteen of us. She hadn't been alone in the kitchen, but it wouldn't have been hard, when no one was looking, to flick a hand and raise the card out of my recipe box long enough to commit the recipe to memory.

"You'll forget what you learned," I said. It wouldn't've taken much to add magic to my words, ensure that what I said came to pass. But in front of everyone, I had to make it Philippa's choice—plus I would never, ever tamper with someone's memory.

Philippa bowed her head. "So mote it be," she murmured.

Everyone breathed out. She'd sworn to forget it; the crisis was over.

Still, I entertained the charming fantasy of making an unholy screeching noise and launching myself across the table, scattering sugary delicacies everywhere, to tackle her.

"Thank you," I said.

Dana's head swung towards the foyer moments before the doorbell rang. The person nearest to the front door opened it, and we heard a chorus of voices.

Ah, the carolers. Every year they came, stubbornly singing their Christian songs. We respected their beliefs—and their tenacity—and were very good about not sniggering if they sang "The Holly and the Ivy," because we knew what it was really about.

I lagged behind as everyone trooped to the door. As soon as the last person was around the corner out of the dining room, I waved a hand over Philippa's fudge and softly spoke a few choice words.

I would never have done anything to Philippa's dessert had she not stolen my secret recipe. It would have been hitting below the broomstick. I wanted to best her fair and square, not by being manipulative with magic. I had *standards*.

I'd meant only to make the fudge taste bad, have a gritty texture, to make people think that even with a simple, tried-and-true recipe, Philippa still couldn't pull it off.

But when everyone trooped back from the carolers and gathered around the table overflowing with desserts, a lot of people reached for the fudge. Let's face it, controversy is sexy. They wanted to find out if Philippa's fudge was as good as mine.

Everyone who sampled the fudge got an…unusual expression on their faces.

It was all I could do to keep from smiling.

But then, one by one, they reached into their mouths and pulled out a small origami crane.

Both Philippa and I flushed. At least, I assumed I did, given the rising heat I felt.

In Celtic mythology, cranes symbolized envy.

Dammit. I *knew* better than to try to cast a spell after a couple of glasses of Pinot Grigio.

Half the partygoers looked at me with pity, and the other half looked at Philippa with the same expression.

Well. That was interesting. At least fifty percent of my friends were on my side. That's what the looks meant, right?

The dessert exchange broke up soon after that. Apparently a good number of people didn't trust *any* of the treats after the crane incident, because I was left with a mountain of cookies. I was able to persuade Maggie to take most of them to school: "At the end of the day I'll sugar up the little bastards and send them home," she said with more glee than she ought to have had.

Dana, who had children in the school, closed her eyes and muttered a string of impressive obscenities.

I didn't blame her. I didn't need precog ability to know we should all be bracing ourselves.

The night of the Solstice was bright and clear, with that blue-black sky that only a winter's night can bring. The snow glittered beneath the dome of sparkling stars. Earth and air, water and fire.

We celebrate our rituals in the park in the center of the neighborhood. The snow was soft underfoot as we crossed the green, and of course our footsteps disappeared as we went. It wasn't brutally cold, although the whole idea of doing a ritual skyclad was clearly made up by people who lived in warmer climates.

So we wore warm boots, thick stockings, heavy skirts and sweaters. Instead of hats, wreaths of holly adorned everyone's heads except for mine and Philippa's, to be burned in the bonfire during the ritual. (Yes, we have a firepit in the middle of our park for ritual purposes. We also have a turf labyrinth, and a communal garden for magical herbs.)

The fire lit, we joined hands in a circle. Thirteen of us, singing praise to the Goddess and the God, our voices rising through the air, visible thanks to the cold. Drawing up energy from the earth and down from the moon.

And so we raised a Circle, invisible to the untrained eye, domed over our heads and beneath our feet. A sacred place.

We dropped hands.

Last night, we'd met, all thirteen of us, and drawn Tarot cards from a deck that couldn't be influenced by magic. A truly random drawing, to see which two witches would lead the ritual this year.

The powers that be showed their sense of humor. Of *course* Philippa and I drew the most powerful cards: the Empress and the High Priestess.

"I'll follow your lead," Philippa had said, and I'd said "I'll email you the plan," which I had. It wasn't much different from past rituals, but she'd extended her olive branch, and I'd extended mine.

Now, she and I stepped to the center of the circle, on one side of the fire, the other women closing the gaps behind us.

Even a few steps closer to the fire changed the temperature. Whew. My body tingled from the combined energy of earth, air, fire, water, and spirit. I felt calm, centered.

Between us was the altar, solid and heavy, carved from an enormous walnut stump generations ago. We each lit a fat white pillar candle, one ringed with holly, the other with oak leaves. Then we each picked up the wreaths. I settled holly on my head; Philippa nestled oak on hers.

I breathed in the crisp snowy air, tasted the smoky scent of the fire. It was exhilarating.

"Now is the time of the winter solstice, the time of darkest night," I said. "The time of the Holly King."

"Yet now, it is also the time of His death," Philippa intoned, "so that he may be reborn at the lightest time of summer."

With each phrase, I felt the energy pulse and grow. But it felt, too, as if we were pushing at each other, even though we weren't physically touching. We should have been sharing, mingling our energies.

"This is a celebration of rebirth," I said. "The Holly King lays down his mantle…"

"…and the Oak King reclaims his," Philippa said.

"The Holly King passes…"

"…and the Oak King is born of the Goddess."

Even though I'd written the bulk of the ritual, when I'd emailed it to Philippa, I'd said I was open to suggestions, and she'd given me some, and I had included them. But now, every time Philippa spoke, I felt as though she was challenging my words, trying to make hers better, stronger. As much as I tried to tamp it down, my annoyance with her grew with every passing moment.

We said the next sentences, but instead of combining our

energy, agreeing, speaking as one, I felt her drawing up more energy and shoving it at me.

"As the Wheel turns, the old king's strength wanes as a new challenger rises to claim the hand of the Goddess," I said. But I was thinking *No. You don't have more power than me.* I matched her, held my ground, imagining a shield. "The kings of Holly and Oak, of waning and waxing, of dark and light, must do battle on this day."

Philippa's eyes glittered dark in the firelight. She almost sounded sarcastic as she said, "I crown the Holly King, lord of the waning year. Now is the time of your greatest power. Are you ready to do battle for the hand of our Goddess?"

I thought I heard Maggie's voice, so very faint in my head, saying *Kimberly…*, her tone a plea, a warning. I thought I felt something from Dana, which in words would translate approximately to *Oh shitballs.*

If I backed down, Philippa would overwhelm me. The ritual was about balance, and I had to stand my ground, defend myself.

"I crown the Oak King, lord of the waxing year," I said. "Your season is almost upon us. Are you ready to do battle for the hand of our Goddess?"

I spoke the question as an answer to hers: *hell yeah, bring it on.*

In some traditions, people act out the choreographed battle between the two aspects of the God; in others, they reenact the birth of the new God from the loins of the Goddess. We simply raised our hands, closed our eyes, imagined the battle between the Gods and the resurrection of the Oak King.

As one, we knew the moment when the world poised in the very middle of the longest night of the year, about to tip toward the light again.

One by one, going deosil, or sunwise, around the circle,

all thirteen of us tossed our circlets into the fire. The holly was subsumed by the flames from the oak logs, symbolizing the Holly King's darkness submitting to the Oak King's light.

Or, at least, it was supposed to.

Instead, I threw my holly wreath in, the final symbol of the dying Holly King, then Philippa threw in her oak leaf wreath, a symbol of the Oak King triumphing in his blaze of glory…

…but the fire *went out*.

I blinked in the sudden darkness, feeling as if I was coming out of a trance. My sight adjusted to the dim light provided by the candles and the stars and the faint reflection off the snow, but my eyes watered from the smoke billowing from the firepit.

"Uh oh," I said. "That wasn't supposed to happen." I looked at Philippa. Her eyes no longer looked as black, but they were wide with guilt. "What did you do?" I demanded.

"Me?" She reared back. "I didn't bloody do anything. What did *you* do?"

You moved here. But I didn't say it. Instead I took a long, deep breath in, blew it out and watched the air swirl in the cold. "It doesn't matter now. Now we have to fix things." I looked beyond her at the semicircle of women staring at us, then turned around to look at the semicircle behind us.

But they weren't staring at us. None of them were. They were all staring through the trees, down the street. Dana was muttering an impressively blistering string of curses.

I followed their gaze, and felt my stomach drop. Behind me, Philippa gasped.

They were all looking at my house.

My house, with my wonderful rooftop decoration of life-sized Holly and Oak kings battling it out.

Only now they weren't decorations, and they really *were* battling.

Where in Annwn had they gotten *swords*? I hadn't given the figures swords. They were my *holiday decorations*.

Holiday decorations who were going to do some serious damage to my wrought iron widow's walk if they kept this up.

"Okay," I said, raising my voice enough that everyone finally turned to look at me. "Let's figure out how to fix this. Together we can—"

"Oh, no," Dana said, as she and Maggie and the rest of the coven all took a collective step backwards. "This is all on you and Philippa. We had nothing to do with it."

Panic fluttered in my stomach. "No, we were all doing the ritual," I protested, even though I had a growing terror that they were right.

"The bulk of the energy was coming from the two of you," Maggie said.

"And the God took over your decorations," Dana pointed out.

They stepped closer to Philippa and I, and Dana added, quietly, so the rest of the coven couldn't hear, "Look, this happened because the two of you were having a pissing match instead of honoring the ritual. You two need to work it out on your own, between the two of you."

"I don't think there's anything the rest of us can do to help," Maggie added, sotto voce.

"But call us if you need us," Dana added.

Before Philippa or I could protest, they stepped back into the circle of women.

Around us, everyone clasped hands and raised them to the heavens, then slowly brought them down, finally crouching to release and splay their fingers on the snow, releasing the Circle, returning the energy.

I automatically did the same, as did Philippa. Unreleased energy was headache-inducing at best, dangerous at worst.

Still, I was a little miffed that they all dropped the Circle without discussing it with us.

But I also knew Dana and Maggie were right. Philippa and I had done this.

We had to be the ones to fix it.

"Right," I said, pulling my gloves back on, "let's go reclaim the balance and bring back the light."

I wished I felt half as confident as I sounded.

I stomped back out of the village green, Philippa double-timing to catch up. We didn't bother to erase our steps in the snow.

When Philippa caught up to me, she said, "I think the Tarot choosing us to perform the ritual together was a sign."

"You think?" I snapped, then shook my head, swallowing my anger. In a milder tone, I said, "Yes, you're right. There are no coincidences."

"Any theories about why?" she asked.

Well, at least it was nice to be asked, instead of challenged. I no longer felt her energy pushing at me; now, though, it was more of a wall she'd retreated behind. Or maybe a shield. I didn't take much satisfaction in the thought that maybe she was scared of what I might do. A teensy-tiny bit of satisfaction, maybe, because hey, I'm only human, right?

"Not yet," I admitted.

That iota of smugness vanished as we got closer to my house.

I'd made life-sized figures of the two aspects of the God. Now they were...well, maybe life-sized for *them*.

They were huge.

The widow's walk at the top of my house had a wrought-iron railing that hit a little above waist height; probably would've hit Philippa at the waist, given that she's a bit taller than me.

It came to the Gods' knees.

I didn't think there was any way to go up there without being squished or flung off or otherwise suffering some unhappy bodily injury. It wasn't so much that the Gods would turn on us, but that right now, we weren't in their realm of consciousness. Their battle was their battle.

Which was how it always was. We invite the spirits to enter our Circle, join us in our ritual and celebration, but it's not as if they're partying with us on their level.

They're on a whole 'nother level altogether.

"Hey!" I yelled anyway. *"Hey! Knock it off!"*

Philippa stared at me. "Bloody hell," she said, her breath curling around her face. "You're going to get us both killed. You can't speak to them that way!"

"I'm just trying to get their attention," I said.

"And *then* what?" she demanded. "Ask them nicely to settle their differences and shake hands and oh, let one defeat the other because it would be lovely to see the sun rise?"

"Do you have a better plan?" I asked.

She pursed those lush lips together and glanced away. Finally she said, "Not yet. I'm just trying to say that perhaps mortal solutions are less likely to work."

"Because using magic to make things easier is *always* the solution." It came out before I could stop it. It held all of the frustration and anger and, yes, fear that had been caroming inside of me since she showed up, magnified by this much, much bigger problem raging over our heads.

She took a step back as if I'd slapped her, and I felt like an ass.

"I'm sorry," I said, knowing the words were lame. I forced the next words out; I didn't want to say them, but they were true. "We shouldn't be fighting about our problems, because that—" I pointed up, even though neither of us had to look "—needs to be our focus. Let's…let's take a minute to ground and center, then look at our options. No idea gets shot down without consideration."

Her chin went up; her mouth was in a tight line. In the near-darkness, her eyes still seemed huge. Finally, she gave a curt nod. "Very well. Because if we can't figure this out, the sun isn't going to rise."

She tilted her head to the east, and I realized with horror that she was right. By this time, it should have been growing lighter, the black into gray, soon to be the pale pink of deep winter dawn.

There was nothing but the blue-blackness of eternal midnight.

This wasn't about the two of us—this was about bringing back the light for the whole world.

I stared up at the kings of summer and winter, of dark and light, wrestling on the roof of my house. The Oak King seemed to be more of the aggressor; the Holly King, the defender.

I closed my eyes. Drew in a long breath, connected with the energy of earth and sky, just enough to clear my mind and emotions so I could really meditate on the problem. The sounds on the roof—the grunts, the thuds, the twang of wrought iron that was probably going to snap and rain down and impale us—faded.

Lord and Lady, help me see clearly, I thought, and a moment later, clarity slammed upside my head in a cosmic two-by-four of obviousness.

Ow. But I sent a *thank you* into the universe and faced what should have been evident from the start, if only I'd been open enough to see it.

I was like the Holly King, fighting to keep things the same, and Philippa represented the newness of the Oak King. I resisted the transition, the change, because I felt threatened, rather than being open to the knowledge that the Wheel always must turn.

I opened my eyes, turned to Philippa. Because we were half-between the worlds, I saw that oak wreath on her head again, and didn't have to reach up to feel the prick of holly leaves to know my own wreath was there.

"Dana was right," I said. "We did cause this. *I* caused this. I've been jealous of you ever since you moved here, because you represented change, and I wanted things to stay the same. Instead of infusing the energy of transition into the ritual, I resisted—just like the Holly King is doing. And the harder you pushed, the harder I fought back."

"Kimberly," Philippa said urgently, "I respect your standing in the community. I don't want to take over. I just want to share…and learn from you, too."

"Me? What are you talking about?"

"You're right," she said quietly. "I'm not good at many things, and I've always fallen back on magic. But you, you're perfect. Everything you do is at a level I can't even imagine. You *are* magic."

I just…I don't…

"And I've gone about things the wrong way; I see that now," she added. "Of course you felt threatened by me, the way I was acting. I thought I was being neighborly, participating in the potlucks and baking for everyone. But I was using that as an excuse, when really, I wanted people to like me as much as they like you."

Fuck. I wasn't going to say it to Philippa, but maybe I *did* feel like my standing the community was lodged in what I could provide, rather than who I was.

"We're idiots," I said, which provoked a startled laugh from her.

"I do believe we are," she agreed.

"As much as I hate to admit it, this isn't a time for doing things the hard way," I said. "This *is* a time for magic."

We joined hands, and repeated the words of the ritual. It was the time of the Holly King, and the time of his death, and the time of the rebirth of the Holly King into the Oak King, who would bring back the light and lead us towards summer. This time, we didn't oppose with our words or our energies; we spoke together, and the energy flowed back and forth, open.

At the Summer Solstice, the Oak King would step down and make way for the Holly King to return. An eternal cycle.

And all the while, the Goddess watches over all.

For a brief moment, Philippa and I were Goddess, mourning the Holly King while celebrating the Oak King's birth.

The sounds of battle above us faded.

"Look," Philippa whispered.

I opened my eyes.

In the east, the faint tendrils of dawn.

I let out a breath I hadn't realized I'd been holding, relief making me weak-limbed. We dropped hands, released the energy, fingers buried in the snow.

"Well," she said, rising to her feet and brushing off her brown leather gloves, "I'm knackered, and Cecil must be wondering why the ritual's taking so long."

"You two want to come over for dinner tonight?" I asked.

She smiled. "We'd love to—if you'll come over next week."

"Just no peppermint fudge," I said.

She nodded. "Actually, I'd love it if you could teach me to bake. When I try to do it on my own, things burn, collapse, or explode."

"I'll put up a protective shield," I said.

She turned and started to walk away. I almost headed into my house, but instead, I crouched down, scooped up some snow, and nailed her in the middle of the back with a snowball.

With a shriek, she turned, and a moment later I tried to duck one coming at me, but she probably had put just a weak bit of magic in it, because it landed on my forehead, spattering my face with icy cold flakes.

I had no clue where the rest of the coven had been hiding, but the next thing we knew, they were all there, and it was some sort of crazy free-for-all. Even fastidious, dramatic Georgine.

I couldn't remember the last time I'd laughed so hard.

Things were only going to get better. I didn't need Dana's precog abilities to tell me that.

I was going to make things better.

THE REAL HOUSEWITCHES OF CALAFIA COUNTY

THE REAL
HOUSEWITCHES OF
CALAFIA COUNTY
Don't mess with *this* coven!
DAYLE A.
DERMATIS
"...One of the best writers working today."
– USA Today bestselling author Dean Wesley Smith

ABOUT THIS STORY

When the head of their local HoA tries to impose new rules on the annual Winter Solstice ritual, the four reigning witches of the gated community resolve to fight back.

A war consisting of both paperwork and magic.

All without breaking a fingernail.

Don't mess with this coven!

THE REAL HOUSEWITCHES OF
CALAFIA COUNTY

I'D HAD my mani-pedi done to both celebrate the upcoming
holiday and my own backyard: blue that matched the infinity
pool and white for the marble columns that held up the lanai
roof. My high-heeled sandals clicked on the painted concrete
as I set out glasses, an ice bucket, and a pitcher of jalapeño-
lime margaritas. As well as the bottle of white rum, because
Felisha often preferred it on the rocks with a twist of lime.

A few simple appetizers: Dates stuffed with goat cheese
and wrapped in bacon. Crostini with bruschetta made with
tomatoes from my own garden. A vegan white bean and arti-
choke dip with organic chia seed crackers.

It was a balmy seventy-two degrees, without a cloud in
the sky. The city view over the valley with the mountains
beyond was exquisite as always.

Winter Solstice in Southern California was approaching,
and my fellow coven members and I had planning to do.

I was new to the West Coast, new to the neighborhood,
new to the group. My husband was making the transition
from producing Broadway plays to producing movies, and

the differences between NYC and Hollywood were monumental in some ways, minor in others.

Being welcomed into the gated community coven made things easier. I still wanted our get-together to be perfect, though.

The front doorbell chimed, and although the door was unlocked (gated community and all), I still went to answer it.

Vanessa was the first to arrive, as usual. She wore her dark hair up off her neck in a fancy French twist. Her red one-piece bathing suit highlighted her light brown skin and her fake eyelashes highlighted her big dark eyes. Khaki shorts and sandals completed her outfit.

We hugged and air-kissed, even though we'd seen each other earlier that day at spin class.

(Hey, magic can't fix everything, not without consequences. A little glamour is one thing. Hard work at the gym and maybe the occasional nip-and-tuck are required to maintain oneself, witch or no.)

"Come on back," I said. "The others will be here soon."

She adjusted her red leather bag (which matched her suit) on her shoulder. Despite her careful makeup, I could see the dark circles under her eyes, and I could feel her unsettled aura as if she were throwing it at me.

"You need a margarita," I said.

"Goddess, yes!"

I'd just poured her one when the other two arrived.

Felisha, with her mahogany skin, nearly poreless (and that was natural, damn her). She looks like an Egyptian goddess, and unsurprisingly favored those deities in her personal work.

Shay, with her pale skin and long, curly red hair, looking like a Pre-Raphaelite goddess. She bucked fashion (gasp!) by wearing long, flowing skirts, tea-stained lace and pale silks, and floaty scarves (although she ditched the latter when she was working on her jewelry, because trailing scarves tended to scatter beads and catch fire from the soldering iron).

"You'll never believe what she did this time!"

We didn't need to ask who Shay was talking about. We knew: Anastacia, the president of our Home Owner's Association.

Anastacia and her husband had been among the first residents of the community. Her husband had been the hereditary witch and had been influential in forming a neighborhood for our kind. Anastacia had been supportive of him, but she really didn't know as much about us. He'd died years ago and Anastacia, well, she'd been on the HoA board all along, arguing that she'd earned the position.

Shay waved a piece of paper. "She wrote me up for not taking my Samhain decorations down within, and I quote, 'the proscribed time period'."

Felisha frowned. "I don't remember you still having Samhain decorations up."

"Exactly! The besom"—Shay was referring to a witch's ritual handmade broom—"by the front door is something I always display, no matter the season. But she wouldn't budge. I still have to pay her ridiculous fine."

"Okay, why don't you sit down and I'll get you a drink?" I said, leading her to one of the overstuffed white sofas in the outdoor living space by the pool. Vanessa took the cue and dipped a glass in purifying salt before pouring in the margarita mix and garnishing it with a lime.

When Shay gets worked up, she sets things on fire. It's not her fault; fire is her element and passion runs in her veins. But this is Southern California, and the last thing anyone needed was an errant spark that set off a forest fire.

Combined, we likely had the power to put out the fire before it spread, but who wants to take that chance?

Shay took a hefty sip of the margarita, closed her eyes,

and sighed. I felt the worst of the energy flow out of her, dissipating into the air. I flicked my fingers, dispersing it further so it didn't land on an unsuspecting passer-by.

"An it harm non, honey," I said, quoting the Wiccan rede. "An it harm none."

"It's a minor thing in the long run, I know," she said, "but Lord and Lady, she irks me. With the problems I'm having making jewelry, I don't have a lot of extra cash to deal with her petty fines."

Shay designed high-end jewelry, both for the masses and for the pagan community. The pagan jewelry was where she made the bulk of her money, because she imbued each piece with magic depending on what the wearer needed. She had the ability to know what each piece required, and then she could market it accordingly.

But she'd hit early menopause, and the energy surges and hot flashes were seriously dicking with her spellwork.

Imagine trying to film a movie when the generator keeps blowing.

We were all on edge this year, each with something to work through.

Vanessa's ex-husband died in November, and even though he was her ex (cheating, embezzling from his own company), she still had complicated feelings about him, and she wasn't handling his death well. Felisha was dealing with empty nest syndrome and worrying too much about her kids. As for me...

I was the only one without a real problem, honestly. My issues were small beans compared to theirs. I was just... between projects. At loose ends.

I know most people look at us in our cushy gated community and assume we're trophy wives of rich husbands (sometimes true) or living off fat divorces (also sometimes true) who do nothing all day but shop and gossip and have spa days (occasionally true as well). All of that probably describes the *Real Housewives* shows on TV. (I haven't seen them.)

But as witches, along with harming none, we have a responsibility to the world. To nature, to energy, to balance. So we all try to find ways to make the universe a better place.

One of my talents is organization. I mean, I'm scary-good at it. I either go into an existing charity and get them on track, or I start a new one and get it running smoothly…at which point I get bored and move on.

Oh, of course I was helping out with the Winter Solstice ritual, but the girls had it running well already so it wasn't much of a challenge. They also host an associated gala fundraiser for a different charity each year.

But in terms of a new, big project to whip into shape and make run like clockwork? I had nada. Nothing.

The Solstice ritual was going to be in part to bring Vanessa closure, Felisha peace, Shay focus, me clarity and direction. The theme of dark into light worked for everyone.

And nobody, not even Anastacia, was going to dick with us, by the Goddess.

Of course, I didn't expect a notice from the HoA to appear the next morning on *my* kitchen island, either.

I was brewing a cup of sustainable Costa Rican roast and reviewing the instructions our cook had left for us. Because I wasn't yet working full-time, we employed him only three days a week, but he prepped meals for the other nights so all I had to do was assemble and pop things in the oven, essentially.

Or toss enormous salads, which seemed to be a local thing.

Which was a good thing, because unlike most hedge-witches, I didn't have the innate drying-herbs-and-candle-making abilities. Anything more than assembling hors d'oeuvres and mixing drinks was beyond me.

Our kitchen—bigger than my first apartment—is done in tasteful shades of gray. Pale gray granite shot through with darker streaks, stainless steel appliances, and round pendant lamps with round, clear bulbs exposing the filaments.

The room smells of herbs—just because I can't grow them doesn't mean my friends can't donate them—and sunshine from the four high folding doors that lead to an outdoor eating patio.

The HoA notice probably shouldn't have surprised me. After all, we'd received a fine on our very first day, for having our garage door open for more than, oh, one-point-two seconds.

On our first day, when we were *moving in* and the movers needed *access* to the *garage and shit*.

We paid the fine because at that point, we didn't want to rock the boat.

This boat was gonna capsize pretty damn soon.

There was a popping sound like a light bulb blowing out, the briefest odor like a struck match, and the HoA notice was floating down from a spot about a foot above the kitchen island.

My heather-gray, handle-less coffee mug cradled between my palms, I watched, stunned, as the paper settled gently on the island before I could rouse myself to pick it up.

You've got to be kidding me. What now?

I flicked a finger, drawing the paper to me.

According to bylaw number blah de blah, outside rituals of more than three attendees had to be pre-approved by the board.

At first I thought the notice was referring to the Solstice ritual, but why had it come to me when I wasn't in charge.

Then I realized: it was referring to our *meeting* yesterday.

I set down my mug. Carefully. Took a deep breath in through my nose, out through my mouth, grounding.

When I felt centered and calm (mostly calm) again, I called Anastacia.

Even though she'd just sent the notice, I had to leave a message, although she called me back a few moments later. "Hello dear!" she said. She called everyone *dear*. As if that was going to make anyone less cranky. "What can I do for you?

"It's about this notice I just received."

"Which notice is that, dear?"

Another calming breath. I quoted the bylaw number and rule.

"Oh, *that*," she said as if it were nothing. I imagined her waving a hand dismissively. She was the type who wore multiple chunky gold and diamond rings, all gifts from her late husband.

I waited for her to continue, but she didn't.

"It wasn't a ritual," I said finally. "It was a meeting of the Solstice ritual and fundraising committee."

I supposed she could argue that hors d'oeuvres and margaritas were akin to cakes and ale, but…

The real issue was that somehow, she or one of her cronies had looked into my backyard. My private backyard. My backyard that wasn't visible unless you went through a gate and then stood on a box to peer over a wall. Or you used a drone. Or some magical means I didn't even want to think about right now.

"Oh!" Anastacia said. "Sorry about that, dear. Just fill out the appropriate form and turn it in to the board, and we'll review it and reverse the decision."

"A form," I said.

"Yes, it's in the appendix of the bylaws."

As we'd been talking, I'd been heading to my home office. I hadn't done much with the space since we moved in because I hadn't had any good projects to work on. The walls were a soothing sage green and the trim was white. An ergonomic chair and L-shaped mahogany desk looked toward the French doors that led to the rest of the house, with a matching vertical file cabinet against a wall. No knickknacks yet, although a sage bundle sat in a clam shell on the filing cabinet, left over from when I'd smudged the room to purify it.

I jiggled the mouse to wake up my computer screen, and asked, "Are the bylaws online?" I assumed I could fill out the form that way.

"Oh, I'm afraid not. Just one of those things we haven't gotten around to yet." She laughed. I didn't.

"Can I drop by and pick up a copy, then?" Sending me the entire bylaws the same way she'd sent me the notice wasn't worth the expended energy.

"Let me check my schedule." I heard papers rustling, then, "I'm free for the next hour, if that suits you. The cost for a copy of the complete bylaws is three hundred dollars, and I can take a check or cash, but not a credit card. As for the form, you can make a photocopy, but your signature has to be original."

I know that jaw-dropping is a cliché, but when I realized my jaw had indeed dropped, I snapped my mouth shut. This also served to prevent me from blurting out anything I would regret.

For people in this community, three hundred dollars was a drop in the proverbial bucket. I mean, I spend more than that on a decent bottle of wine or dinner for two at Normandie. Our monthly HoA fee was more than that.

You'd think the fee would include a copy of the bylaws, but apparently not.

There wasn't a branch of our bank near our house, so I logged in to the bank's website, said a few words, and transferred out three hundred dollars in hundred-dollar bills. They appeared on my desk.

I yawned. The spell had taken enough energy out of me that I needed at least one more cup of coffee before I went to see Anastacia.

Gods and Goddesses, I hated this kind of unnecessary, over-layered bureaucracy.

The bylaws were gathered in a black three-ring binder with a two-inch spine. The binder smelled every so faintly of mildew, and the pages inside had been photocopied multiple times. For three hundred dollars, I'd have expected something a little…classier. And a new printout. And a bottle of wine.

Pity it was too early to start drinking

Back in my home office, I flipped through the pages to find the relevant section. The numbers, though, ended before they reached the particular bylaw I was looking for. A note at the end of the section said that bylaws added since this edition could be found…

Morrigan's breath, you had to be kidding me.

Found *online*.

So while the bulk of the bylaws were still paper only, all of the additions and amendments were digital.

Not the form I needed, mind you. It existed only in the notebook, copied so many times it was faint and crooked.

Basically, it gave a space for me to explain why the infraction I'd been charged with wasn't really an infraction. (There was also a typo on it.)

I copied it one more time, but I didn't fill it out or sign it.

I went to law school, although I hadn't taken the bar either in New York or here. But one thing I knew was this: you don't sign a contract unless you understand it and agree with it.

I really wanted it to be time for a drink, but I sighed and got myself a lemon-infused soda water and went to work. Starting with page one of the damn bylaws.

The pages weren't numbered properly, due to various inserts, so I had no idea how much I'd read when I was done. At least two hundred pages, which were now bristling with Post-It notes. Then I turned my attention to the additions and addendums and appendices online.

A few moments later, I realized I had to print those out, too, so I could mark them up.

The bylaws were a jumble of information that no longer applied, and conflicting rules and regulations, including new rules that contradicted old rules, and so forth. Instead of reviewing the bylaws when new laws were made, the new laws had simply been slapped on the end (or, for the past ten years or so, online).

And some of those new laws…

I texted the girls, and made plans for lunch the next day.

If we were going to get together to talk about this problem, we were going to do it well away from our houses and the potential for prying eyes.

Before we left, we raised wards around our cars, and we each wore one of Shay's protective amulets, which were also designed to alert us if any other magic was used nearby.

We were probably being silly and overdramatic, but witches haven't survived as long as they have by letting their guard down.

This wasn't an inquisition, of course, but it felt like we were planning a skirmish and you don't go into war without armor, do you?

We'd picked a restaurant near the harbor, and took a table on the back patio, which was otherwise empty of patrons. Our heels clicked on the wooden floor as we made our way to our table, which was shaded by a big cloth umbrella. After taking our drink orders, the waiter left, leaving us with the sound of the breeze through the leaves of the plants providing privacy and the call of the gulls overhead. From the harbor came the twin scents of brine and diesel fuel.

We kept our conversation to lighter things—some Solstice fundraising news, some gossip—while we ate. After I finished my seared ahi salad and the waiter had whisked my plate away, I dropped the binder on the table with a thud.

The other three stared at it, astonished.

"How did we not know about this?" Shay asked.

"We never cared," Vanessa said with a sigh. "I know when we first moved in, it wasn't much of a problem. But Anastacia had just joined the board; she hadn't stepped up as president."

"Complaints started ramping up after that," Felisha said.

"How long has she been president?" I asked.

Vanessa pursed her crimson lips, frowning just enough to not wrinkle her forehead but still conveying her emotion. "About five years?"

"Closer to ten, I think," Felisha said.

"I remember her questioning me about having a home business," Shay said. "Yeah, eight or nine."

"She never gets voted off?" Maybe I don't understand how HoAs work.

Felisha shrugged. "Guess the rest of the board is happy not to have the responsibility."

"Like I said, we've never been to a meeting," Vanessa added.

"Well, we might just need to go to the next one," I said. "It's the last one before Solstice, and I have some serious questions about their newest regulations."

I flipped open the book, paging through until I was close to the end where the most recent regulations were listed.

"For example, look at this," I said, pointing. "'Solstice rituals are prohibited from including interaction with the dead, as that is reserved for Samhain.' We were going to use our smaller ritual to help you gain closure from Vanessa's husband's death. It can't be a coincidence that this was voted in last month." It helped that the regulations were dated, because I hadn't had the chance to ask Anastacia for copies of meeting minutes. Those probably cost a kidney.

Not all the stupid rules related to witchcraft. California had water-rationing laws in place, but our lawns were required to be green (not to mention a specific height in inches) and our cars were required to be clean (even though they weren't allowed to be parked in our driveways for more than fifteen minutes at a time). The drain on magic to make these things happen could be exhausting—long-term spells were much harder on the body and psyche than one-off magics.

Other regulations had specific rules similar to the one about communicating with the dead at Solstice, such as when holiday decorations (for any holiday) could go up and when they had to be taken down. We were required to use cool white instead of warm white LEDs for outside decoration. (I hadn't realized there were two different kinds—my husband was going to have to go through our garage to find out which ones we had.)

Proscriptions about rituals, and what was appropriate for certain ones. Fire safety made sense, of course, but the height of one's altar? What color your gazing ball was?

I was sort of surprised there was nothing regarding whether it was okay to worship while skyclad, but many witches don't believe being naked is a requirement, so perhaps it had never come up.

Or maybe rules about nudity in one's own backyard would raise everyone's hackles, because if you wanted to tan all over…

Plus if they made a rule like that, how would they enforce it without being seen as voyeurs? (If they *did* make up some regulation about that, you'd better believe I'd be having sex with my husband by the pool on a regular basis.)

But I was getting distracted.

"Basically, it looks as though they've been ramping up on things for years," I said, "but the last year or so they've been firing off new rules left and right. I wonder why."

"Isn't it obvious?" Felisha said, turning her dark gaze on me. "It's you."

Shay gasped. "Of course."

Vanessa murmured an assent as well.

"*Me?* What did *I* do?"

"You moved here eight months ago," Felisha said. "Antastacia is threatened by you. It's not anything you did. It's how powerful you are."

My head felt light, as if I'd consumed many more mimosas than I had. This was ridiculous. "I'm not that powerful," I protested.

"You are," Shay said. Her silver and bead bracelets jangled

as she reached out to put a soft, cool hand over mine. "You're the strongest witch in the community."

Vanessa leaned forward, and I felt the power behind her words rise before she even started speaking. "Magic is all about intention and focus, and those are two things you're very, very good at in any situation," she said.

"I'm—" I caught myself before I repeated myself, and changed it to a simple, "Thank you."

"Don't thank us," Shay said. "It's just the truth."

"But Anastacia isn't a hereditary witch," I protested. "We don't even have the same type of power. It's like eye of newt and toe of frog."

Shay snorted.

"Doesn't matter to people like her," Felisha said. "She might even be equating her power in the HoA with your power. Either way, I'm willing to bet my best athame that she sees you as some sort of threat."

"What's she trying to gain, then?" I asked. "A lot of these regulations don't target me specifically.

"True," Vanessa said. "Good question. All the more reason to go to the next meeting."

"Agreed," I said. "I'm not going to go in as an antagonist, but I'll definitely have my shields up."

The final HoA meeting of the year took place the following week. We had a week and a half until the big Solstice ritual and fundraiser, so we were already busy enough. As the day of the meeting grew closer, I found myself wanting to go less and less.

Too much work, I told myself. Plus I wanted to spend the evening with my husband. I wanted to order in and put our feet up and catch up on our Netflix shows, not freshen my makeup and go out.

Maybe we were overthinking things, assuming ulterior motives when there were really none to be found. We could go next month, right?

The others could go without me, I decided, but when I texted them, I discovered they were all feeling tired, worn down, reluctant to go.

Sure, Solstice was coming up soon, but we had things well in hand. It was too much of a coincidence that we were *all* dragging our heels.

I called them up via SkyCall, the witches' version of Skype. (Any clear mirror will suffice.)

"It's a spell," I said. "I asked around last week, and I couldn't find anybody who goes to the meetings except for the board. They have to be putting up an avoidance ward or something."

Vanessa shook her head. "Why didn't I think of that?"

"None of us did," Felisha said. "So let's fight this spell. Shay?"

"Bring your amulets over tomorrow and we'll add extra protection to them, with an emphasis on creating a counter-spell," Shay said immediately. She winked. "We'll do it inside to avoid Peeping Toms."

Or a watching witch…

The four of us stood in a semicircle on the sidewalk, facing Anastacia's house. The doorway to the three-story Mediter-ranean-style house was brightly lit with wrought-iron sconces, and matching solar sconces lined the walkway.

We could feel the nudge of the spell surrounding the

house, encouraging us to walk away, go find something else to do. It wasn't menacing or dangerous, just a pushback.

I hadn't felt it the day I'd picked up the HoA binder, which was in my large, burgundy Prada tote. She must have either dropped the spell when she knew I was coming over, or set it up a few days before each meeting.

I squared my shoulders. "Let's do this," I said.

The others nodded and fell into line behind me. I hadn't intended to take the lead or take point on this mission, but I suppose it made sense. Anastacia seemed to have a problem with me, so I might as well be in charge of facing her.

When Anastacia opened the door, she blinked in surprise at the four of us standing there.

"Oh!" she said. "Oh…hello, dears. How can I help you?"

She was wearing a chic off-white pantsuit and her usual chunky gold jewelry. Her hair was the pale blond older women turn to when they're pretending they aren't really going gray, and perfectly coiffed. I smelled Nag Champa, the incense of witches around the world.

"We're here for the meeting," I said.

Her blue eyes narrowed, just slightly. I had no idea if she sensed the anti-spell wards on our amulets, but if she did, she didn't say or do anything. Pasting on a clearly fake smile, she stepped back and said, "Of course! Come in, dears."

The Mediterranean theme carried inside, unsurprisingly. Vaulted ceilings with exposed, dark wood beams made the place seem vast, especially with the floor covered with broad terra-cotta-hued tiles that made sounds louder.

The formal living area was off to the left and two wide steps down. A large, carved wooden pentagram hung over the stuccoed fireplace. The six other board members sat in a semicircle of coffee-brown leather sofas and overstuffed chairs. All had equally surprised looks on their faces, but stood to exchange air kisses with us.

Anastacia stood looking discomfited, until one of the members—Adam, a retired professional baseball player/current entrepreneur—grabbed some padded straight chairs from around what looked like a gaming or tea table. There wasn't really room to put them between the other furniture, so we sat a little behind, able to see through the gaps.

As we'd suspected, nobody else from the community came to the meetings on any regular basis.

The plus side was, other than Anastacia's reaction, I didn't get the sense from the rest of the members that they were uncomfortable with us being here. My gut said they didn't know what Anastacia had been doing—or if they did, they weren't fully on board with it.

They did a brief energy ritual to seal a Circle around us, and Anastacia called the meeting to order. Most of the meeting was the usual business stuff: reviewing the minutes from last month, authorizing funds to drain and clean one of the ponds, someone's lawn not up to code, double toil and trouble, etc.

"One final vote tonight, and then we can wrap things up," Anastacia said. She hadn't looked at me or the girls since the meeting had started, her gaze skimming past us when she looked at the other board members. "As we discussed briefly last month, we'd like to make a change to the following regulation." She rattled off a number. I paged quickly through the binder but before I could find the relevant part, she went on. "The charity benefitting from the Winter Solstice fundraiser must be at least approved six months prior to the date of the ritual and fundraiser, effective immediately. All in favor?"

All four of us gasped. My hand shot up, and Anastacia was forced to acknowledge me. She kept her face composed and even sounded vaguely pleasant when she said, "Yes, dear?"

She probably thought she had the board in the palm of her hand.

"Aren't you supposed to open the floor for comments and questions before someone makes a motion and someone else seconds it and then you vote?"

I made it sound innocent, but here was the thing: I know *Robert's Rules of Order* better than I know some of our sacred texts. This *was* the hill I was willing to die on, metaphorically speaking.

"Well, yes, of course," she said, now looking annoyed. "But I think we know how we're all going to vote."

"I'm open to discussion," Adam said, looking at me. It was possible he was flirting with me. Well, I'd flirt back if it meant I'd win his vote, but I'd rather it didn't come to that.

Vanessa spoke up. "We announced the charity, Milo's Sanctuary, at Samhain as usual. That's been the procedure for years."

"Plus if you're going to change a rule, it shouldn't be retroactive," Felisha added. "The new regulation shouldn't take effect until the following year."

"If it even passes," Shay chimed in.

"What's the reason behind the proposed change?" I asked.

Anastacia said something about the board wanting more time to review the choice.

"Has the board ever rejected a suggested charity?" Felisha asked. "It hasn't in my memory. Or has the board had an issue with a charity after the fact?"

"I'd have to check the minutes," said Mary Anne, the board secretary. "But I think not."

"A lot can happen in six months," I said. "I can see asking for a list of suggestions by the Summer Equinox, with any reservations or concerns returned to the committee by, say, Lammas. Then we can handle any coordination and have things locked in by Samhain."

"Why don't we table this until next month, so we have time to investigate and consider this new information," Adam suggested. "That way the change wouldn't be retroactive and affect this year, too."

"Is that a motion?" Anastacia asked. Adam nodded.

"Seconded," Mary Anne said.

The vote to table the discussion passed, with Anastacia grudgingly raising her hand when she saw the entire board disagreed with her. She was clearly furious, but holding herself together.

I was just grateful that she couldn't literally shoot daggers from her eyes.

Anastacia tried to end the meeting, but I raised my hand again and said I had a question. She formally recognized me (I didn't even get a "dear"). I said I'd brought my form to protest the write-up of having an unsanctioned ritual of more than four people, since we hadn't been having a ritual, but a planning meeting.

"We enforce that?" one of the board members said with surprise, but I didn't catch who.

Anastacia ignored that question and tersely asked me what mine was. I asked how the board had received the information when my backyard wasn't visible from the street or by my neighbors.

Anastacia sputtered and demurred, finally citing an anonymous tip. I knew, from reading the entire poorly photocopied binder, that anonymous tips were acceptable (to keep the peace, so one neighbor doesn't know which neighbor tattled on them). I could have argued that that anonymous person had broken the law— as in, state or federal law—but I let it go because Anastacia was already accepting my form and canceling my fine.

We'd won a couple of battles, but not the war. And I still wasn't even sure what the war was about.

Anastacia kept quiet in the days leading up to the Solstice. At least, she didn't contact the four of us. We weren't sure whether to be relieved or concerned.

She might have something planned during the ritual or fundraiser, and we were determined that she wasn't going to ruin the holiday.

Solstice Eve held a hint of welcomed crispness, with a clear sky sparkling with stars. (The community walls had an ongoing spell built in that reduced light pollution from the surrounding cities.) Although I'd been enjoying the escape from winter, the closer the holiday came, the more I missed snow, or at least December weather. Winter Solstice in New York City was (pardon the pun) magical in the glittering snow.

One of the other residents in the community owned a high-end party planning firm, which had been hired for years to handle the decorations. I had no reference to what previous years had been like, but this year the community hall was stunning.

The main room, where the ritual would be performed, had been turned into a winter forest wonderland, a sacred grove for sacred rituals. The trees, which covered the walls and grew over the edges of the ceiling, looked and felt real, the bark rough, the branches of the oak and ash stark, the yews and hollies lush green and dotted with red berries.

Above, the ceiling showed the midnight-blue of twilight, with a crescent moon and stars. The room smelled of loam and pine, and I would have sworn the leaves were rustling.

In the center of the room, a rough-hewn stone altar

carved with spirals, and on the altar, the tools of our trade: chalice and athame, wand and bundle of dried sage and lavender.

Despite the insistence that I was the most powerful witch in the community, it had never been in the plan to have me officiate the Solstice ritual. I was too new to the area. And I was perfectly fine with that.

The rest of the community entered the room, forming concentric circles. The thirteen of us followed, carrying unlit, fat white pillar candles, and the circles parted to allow us into the center. I felt odd being in the core thirteen, but everyone else had welcomed me warmly. We walked around the altar three times, then twelve of us formed a final circle with Felisha, serving as High Priestess for the evening, in the center next to the altar.

We set the candles in a ring around the altar, and straightened.

We were in the sacred space that we all had created. Magic hummed as each woman drew power from the earth and sky. For me, it was like a tingling just under my skin, and a sense of pure joy.

This was the community-wide ritual, whereas later, Vanessa, Shay, Felisha, and I would have a private one, to work on our personal issues—HoA rules or not.

Given what we'd been dealing with in the past few weeks, we'd made minor modifications to this ritual. Winter Solstice was the longest night of the year, the shortest day. It was a celebration of the coming longer days, the Wheel turning and bringing us spring, and new growth, and also a reflection of the past year and a farewell to the seasonal darkness. It was a time of letting go of something negative, and letting in something positive—things individual to each person.

We as witches were also guardians of the earth. We were responsible to nature, to energy, to balance.

Given not only the recent events but what had been going on in the world at large, we'd realized we needed to bring everyone together and call up energy for a greater purpose.

Felisha, with her melodious voice, guided us through the opening stages of the ritual: the calling of the guardians of the four directions; dipping the blade into the chalice to honor the balance of feminine and masculine, Goddess and God; honoring the Holly King who dies this night, and welcoming the Oak King who will usher us into summer.

"Winter Solstice," Felisha said. "The Wheel turns. Darkness into light. In our homes, and around the world, witches will banish something negative, something holding them back, and embrace something positive to bring into the growing light and embody in the coming year."

"So mote it be," the rest of us intoned.

"Here, though, we gather together for greater purposes. We are the guardians of the Earth, our Mother. We are the protectors of her flame, and we champion her when she is in need."

"So mote it be."

"To do that, we care for each and every person. We are all connected. We are all imperfect, but we are all worthy. Guarding the Earth, our Mother, starts here, with each other. Here, in this community, and the country, and across the world."

"So mote it be."

Everyone in the room was raising energy. Through our clasped hands and through our hearts, we sent it deosil, clockwise, left hand to right. In the end, we'd release it out into the world, sending it where it needed to go, to people in crisis, to land in crisis.

When Felisha said *community*, however, the four of us nudged some extra energy at Anastacia, trying to underscore the point.

We hoped it would weaken her hold on the community—more by giving everyone strength to resist the compulsions she brewed—but also remind her that community was more important than the individual. We didn't attack, except with love and compassion.

Anastacia nudged back.

I glanced around the inner circle. Nobody else seemed to have noticed. The nudge had been for me personally.

I hadn't wanted to do this alone. I'd really, really hoped Anastacia would get the message, take the hint, see that she was focusing in the wrong direction.

But the others had been right: for some reason, I was on her personal shit list.

The Circle we'd raised was supposed to be a safe place, a space of love and trust. For that reason, none of us were wearing our amulets; they would have been counter to the energy here.

We never thought Anastacia would act out here, during the ritual.

I reached inside for a protection spell, a way to raise shields around myself that wouldn't block the flow of the energy swirling in the room but that would give me a barrier against Anastacia, but I was too late.

The world tilted, sideways and back again, and I was no longer in the room.

I was no longer in my *body*.

Well, that was a little disconcerting.

The astral plane was everything and nothing, black and white and every color and yet no color at all. Because I had no body, I didn't have the five normal bodily senses. Everything was *feeling*, an inner sense rather than an outer one.

Hereditary witches know the astral plane instinctively. I had no idea where or how Anastacia had learned to access it.

Why? I asked. *What did I ever do to you?*

No response.

I'm not your enemy, I added. *None of us are. Is there something you need—?*

Something slammed into me, or, rather, into my noncorporeal consciousness. Then a jerk, as if she was trying to pull something out of me.

Energy. Power.

She wanted it, I had it.

Oh, she wanted to play this game, did she?

She had more power than she should have, certainly, but she was no match for me. I responded in kind, reaching out with tendril non-fingers and delving into the part of her that was in the astral plane.

I latched on to her core, the place where power was stored. And I pulled.

She shrieked without sound and yet I somehow heard it. She struggled against me, fought to stop me from dragging the power out of her, hand over hand like pulling up an anchor, but she didn't have the knowledge or the skill.

I pulled her power to me, wrapped it into a ball that in my mind's eye glowed gold and silver both, and kept packing it tighter and smaller until I could "carry" it with me.

I didn't take everything—the last thing I wanted to do was cause her harm, either astrally or physically. But I took enough that apparently she could no longer hold us here.

I came back to my body with a jolt, stumbling with one foot forward before pulling myself together (literally). Felisha shot me a concerned look, and I raised my chin in a nod to let her know I was okay.

I couldn't see Anastacia—she'd been somewhere in the crowd behind me. The ritual was continuing, and I had to focus on it.

Felisha urged us to increase the flow of energy through our bound hands, faster and faster until it began spiraling up.

As one, we released our grips and raised our hands up, firing the magic up into the world, to land where it was most needed.

When we did that, I sent Anastacia's power along with my own and everyone else's, choosing to spread it through our community or beyond.

After all, that was the point of having magic.

❦

Anastacia had scurried out the door as soon as the Circle was lowered. We focused on the refreshments and the fundraiser, which went very well indeed.

The next day, she was gone. Her house was empty, and before long a For Sale sign appeared on the yellowing lawn.

Slowly, over the next month or two, facts and information trickled in, allowing us to piece together the overall picture.

It turned out Anastacia had developed a bit of a gambling problem after her husband died. She'd been skimming off the HoA dues as well as the more frequent fines for new violations. The other board members hadn't even known about some of the violations and fines she'd levied, meaning those funds had gone directly into her pocket.

On top of that, she'd been getting off on the power of being in control, of policing the community. As in, it had been allowing her to increase her magical abilities to the level of a hereditary witch. She'd always felt left out, lesser, and when her husband died, that had turned into something of an obsession. Apparently she thought the increased power would help her with the aforementioned gambling.

In our private ritual on Winter Solstice night, Vanessa found closure with her dead ex-husband, Shay found ways to control her menopausal energy surges, and Felisha came to Goddess about her kids having grown up and moved away.

Me? I'd already solved my own problem. I needed a project.

And the HoA needed an interim president to clean up the mess Anastacia had made.

All that, and I didn't even break a nail.

A WITCH IN TIME

A WITCH IN TIME
Don't mess with this coven!
DAYLE A. DERMATIS
"...One of the best writers working today."
– USA Today bestselling author Dean Wesley Smith

ABOUT THIS STORY

Witch Dana despairs when her daughter, Ember, says she doesn't want to join the local coven.

So Dana calls on the best person to school her daughter: her dead mother.

Now Dana's off on a magical mystery tour through time.

Hopefully when she returns, she'll have a different outlook on what it means to be a witch.

A WITCH IN TIME

Dana

The kitchen of my Tudor-style house smelled of ginger and cinnamon and cloves, thanks to the cookies in the oven and the ones cooling on the racks, nearly ready for decorating. I opened my box of cookie cutters, each season's or holiday's cutters organized in their own, smaller boxes, and pulled out the ones for the Winter Solstice.

Stars (five-pointed stars are pentagrams, dammit, no matter what the non-pagans think), pine trees (we had them first, dammit), bells to ring in the growing light (ahem, dammit), mistletoe, and of course holly and oak leaves to symbolize the two Kings who would battle on Solstice Night.

The kitchen had oak beams on the ceiling, a rounded-top, Gothic-arch-carved door leading to the dining room, a white porcelain double-farmhouse sink, and a proper British Aga. Far better than those stainless steel monstrosities.

My pre-cog ability told me the cookies were ready a few seconds before the timer, so I was already sliding the tray out of the oven when the chime went off.

"

I slid the cookies onto a cooling tray, hung up my William Morris–patterned oven mitts, and hung my Good House-witching apron on a hook. Time to collect my daughter, Ember, for the annual decorating fest.

Normally our coven, or at least some of us, would get together for the job (nobody had kitchen space for all thirteen of us), but this year was special. Ember had turned fifteen, and was ready to be welcomed into the coven to officially learn our ways.

I knocked on her door, and heard her muffled response to come in.

She lounged on her white-metal twin bed bed in a pair of heather-grey leggings and an oversized dark red sweater that draped almost to the ends of her fingers. White earbuds. Burgundy wool socks with hedgehogs on them.

She had my features—sharp cheekbones, enormous blue eyes, and hair that naturally fell in ringleted curls, only hers were long and currently piled atop her head, whereas I kept mine shoulder length—but she had her father's height.

Given that I was small and slender, people often told me I looked like a fairy, a notion I immediately dispelled when I opened my mouth. I curse like a drunken Scottish warlock (sometimes even with the accent).

People don't expect that.

"Time for cookie decorating!" I said.

Without looking up from her phone, Ember tapped her earbuds to turn them off and said, "No thanks."

I blinked. What the Goddess?

"But it's special this year," I said. "Just you and me, so we can talk about things."

By *things* I meant details of her entry into the coven, which she already knew was coming.

She sat up, rearranging herself so she was sitting cross-legged. "It's not that I don't respect your religion, Mom…" she began.

Hold on. *My* religion?

I should've expected something like this, but I'd accepted her excuses the past few weeks: studying for finals, holiday concert practice, a couple of parties.

But now it was the holiday break…

She shrugged dramatically, with a sigh and roll of her head. Of course she did. Find me a teenager, and I'll find you somcone who shrugs dramatically.

"What do you think we do on the Sabbats and Esbats?" I tried. "Why we light candles, leave out offerings, bless the house for protection?"

"Mom, c'mon," she said. "What you and your friends do— it's just Witchcore."

"Witchcore?"

"Like Cottagecore, or Normcore, or Cabincore. It's an aesthetic. Decorating and clothes and candles and 'spells'."

I could hear the quote marks around "spells." I stiffened.

"It's more than that," I said.

"It's just an esthetic with magical icing on top," she said. "So you can tell who's at the door before they knock and keep lasagne from burning." She shrugged. "You won't even use whatever it is to clean the house or make things easier. You certainly don't use it to make the world a better place."

Even as my ire rose, I realized where she was coming from. As the rest of us had with our children, as my own mother had done with me, I'd deliberately kept her innocent of the responsibilities and duties of being a witch. I'd wanted her to have a childhood—a certain amount of innocence, I suppose—before I burdened her.

That was what today was supposed to begin. An initiation, albeit a gentle one, into what being a witch really meant.

"You think we don't use our powers for good?"

"Sure, sometimes you help others, but really, what's the point? I'd rather do hands-on charity work. I'm already stuffing envelopes and stuff at Planned Parenthood."

My little do-gooder. She'd always been kind, since kindergarten when she took all the kids who were scared or crying under her wing.

Unfortunately, when she defended the less-strong, she had a habit of, er, using some of my words. The talk about her swearing with the teacher and principal had *not* been fun.

"You can do both, you know," I said.

"Look at your friends," Ember continued, ignoring me. "Having a feud over who decorates for the Solstice better. Last year's party was *so* embarrassing."

Philippa's entry to our neighborhood and coven had been rocky. She and my best friend, Kimberly, had gone head-to-head over who was the best at, well, pretty much everything. From holiday gifts to decorating to hosting parties, and more.

There had been a kerfluffle at the annual holiday party at Kimberly's when it turned out Philippa had "borrowed" Kimberly's coveted family fudge recipe.

Ember wasn't wrong. It hadn't been pretty.

The energy of their simmering feud blew up at the Winter Solstice ritual, when the Oak and Holly king life-sized figures on Kimberly's roof came alive with the spirits of the two Gods. Kimberly and Philippa had to work together without anger to calm everything down.

They were cautious friends now, still negotiating who got to do what, and when. Philippa, for example, got Samhain as one of her holidays to shine, while Kimberly had the Winter Solstice to reign over.

I cleared my throat. "Is this something you've been thinking about long?"

"Isla and I have been talking," she said. "She thinks the same thing."

Isla was Ember's best friend and Philippa's daughter.

Ah, I understood what was going on. Ember was a teenager. She was finding her own path, and finding like-minded allies.

Ember—and Isla, apparently—just didn't have all of the information they needed.

I could sit Ember down and explain everything—but if she had given this so much thought, her reaction would be to dig in and double down. She wouldn't hear what I tried to tell her, tried to explain.

I had to handle this a different way.

"Okay," I said. "For now. We'll talk again, okay?"

Ember shrugged, but gave me a smile before she popped her earbud back in.

I knew she and I weren't in the right place to deal with this.

I knew I had to call in the big guns.

But first I was going to call Philippa to warn her that she would probably be having to deal with Isla, if she hadn't already.

At the back of the house we had an attached conservatory. More Victorian than Tudor, it was pentagonal, a story and a half tall, made of glass with black iron supports. It brimmed with plants: herbs both medicinal and culinary, hanging pots of trailing ivy, and urns filled with holly and lady's mantle and foxglove.

It was a cloudy mid-December day, but the room was warm and moist thanks to the plants. I breathed in the green, loamy, life-filled air.

I rolled back the rug in the center to reveal a large penta-gram etched into the flagstone floor and painted a shim-mering gold. I gathered five fat white candles from around the room and placed them at the points, then snapped my fingers to light them.

I settled myself in the middle of the star.

"You told me this day would come, Mom," I said with a sigh. "You cursed me with the 'just wait until you have a daughter' spell, and I'm sorry I didn't listen."

Then I began the ritual to have an oh-so-exciting chat with my deceased mother.

Ember

I woke suddenly, for a reason. Before I moved, I sent out feelers, inspecting the space around me. Mom had warded the house from negative energy (whatever that meant), but that didn't mean something couldn't go wrong.

Be wrong.

Something else here. I breathed in, out.

Sensed no bad intent.

Cautiously, I opened my eyes.

A hazy, glowing figure sat in my desk chair. I slowly sat up, and the figure resolved into a familiar form.

All of my tension melted away. "Grandma!"

"Ember, my sweet."

I didn't know how death worked, exactly; where people-slash-souls went, or how they came back occasionally. My grandmother looked younger than I remembered, or maybe just smoothed out. Fewer wrinkles, more youthful. Her pure white hair was plaited into a thick braid that fell over her shoulder, revealing silver earrings that were tiny wind-chimes. She wore jeans and a T-shirt that said "Styx" in a stylized font, although it didn't depict the river of Hades.

"Did Mom send you?" I asked as my sleep-fogged brain cleared.

"Now, why would you think that?" Grandma asked. "Can't a grandmother visit her granddaughter to check in?"

"You haven't 'checked in' since you died."

"Are you sure about that?" Grandma winked.

I remembered dreaming about my grandmother soon after she'd died, about how Grandma had so often sat at the foot of my bed, and in my dream I swear I'd *felt* the mattress depress.

And how I'd smelled my grandmother's special blend of wild rose and tobacco-leather scent, like an old-fashioned gentleman's study— when no one was around.

Maybe they hadn't been dreams, exactly, after all.

"Okay, no," I confessed. "But why now?"

Grandma drummed her fingers on the arm of the chair.

"I need to show you some things. About our family, and our history. I could tell you, but it wouldn't be the same as seeing it."

I narrowed my eyes. "Which means what, exactly?"

"Well…how familiar are you with *Doctor Who*?"

"Not time theory." I groaned. "I hate time theory. It makes my head hurt."

"One way of looking at it is that time is a river. We step out and stand in the river at any point we choose.…"

I groaned again and clutched my head.

Grandma considered, then gestured at the floor. The socks I'd toed off before bed, three shoes, one shirt, my tablet, my game controller, and a chair all moved out of the way, leaving an open area. Another wave of her hand, and a glowing golden circle appeared on the wooden planks.

Like the One Ring, but without the fancy Elven script. This one had symbols at the four quarters—the two solstices and two equinoxes—and in between each quarter—the four cross-quarter days.

The pagan Wheel of the Year.

"Go ahead, stand in the middle."

This was familiar; it was how we celebrated the year. When we created a ritual space, we turned in all four directions to call spirits or guardians of those quarters. I stepped inside, facing the Winter Equinox—we were close enough to that date. Nothing happened. I looked at my grandmother.

Granma flicked a finger, and the circle began to move deosil, or clockwise, turning in the direction of the sun. "See? You're the center. You don't move. The Wheel moves around you. Time moves around you. When you're alive, it's really hard to see and understand."

"Tell me about it," I murmured. I felt a frisson of energy traveling up from the earth and into her. I was grounding automatically, without thinking about it. I let the energy move through me and out the top of my head. It sort of made sense, but only if I didn't think about it too hard.

"Those of us who've moved on can grok it, though. And use it."

The circle stopped moving and faded into the floor.

"Come along," Grandma said, holding out her hand. "We're off on our magical mystery tour."

"Our *what* now?"

She stopped in her tracks and rolled her eyes. "Sweet Goddess. Your lack of musical knowledge is appalling. When we get back, I'm going to have words with your mother."

Ember

I found myself in space—or what looked like space. Blackness all around, pricked with pinpoints of glittering white light. I made the mistake of looking down and involuntarily clutched my grandmother's hand, then cursed myself for it.

Both for the clutching and the mistake of looking down.

We weren't standing on anything. I still felt as if I were standing, but it looked as though we were floating in the midst of the sky.

I didn't feel air on my skin, but I was somehow breathing. I was thankful there was no real smell, except something she could maybe describe as freshness. Like crisp, cold winter air.

Just not cold, or warm. Neutral.

Then, to make things worse, the stars began to move. Space *rotated*, which it just shouldn't do. Deosil, like the Wheel of the Year. My stomach lurched.

"Take a deep breath," Grandma said. "Another. There you go."

The nausea subsided. Although I still didn't look down again, or up. I decided to pretend I was in a planetarium, even though they made me dizzy and nauseated sometimes, too.

"Time," Grandma said. "We're in the center of it, as it moves around us."

"If you say so," I murmured. Speaking, I worried, would make my stomach somersault again.

"So like I said, I'm going to show you some things," Grandma said. "Ready?"

"Do I have a choice?" I asked, but my grandmother was already raising her free hand and making a slashing-down motion.

A crack appeared in front of us, and pure white light poured out. I barely had time to shield my eyes before Grandma tugged me along again, stumbling, this time through the rend.

∼

Ember

We were in what looked like a courtroom, only old. A middle-aged woman stood behind a half-height dark wood wall, her hands resting on the edge. She was clearly wearing a corset, and over it a high-necked black dress. Her dark blond hair was pulled back, nothing fancy. A working-class woman.

Even from here I could see the exhaustion in her posture, the drawn skin around her mouth, her very energy.

"We can watch, but we can't interact," Grandma said. "No one can hear or see us. Probably a safety measure so we don't destroy life as we know it."

Which also explained why my pajamas and her jeans weren't freaking anyone out.

"I get that part. Step on a butterfly, yadda yadda. But I know about the Salem Witch Trials," I said, sighing. "Ergot poisoning—not witchcraft or devil worship or magic."

"Seriously?" Grandma said. "Pay attention. Does this look like sixteen-nineties Massachusetts to you?"

Oh. No, actually, it did not.

Assumption, my mother was fond of saying, makes an ass out of you and me. I think she just enjoyed saying the word "ass." It was tame compared to some of her vocabulary.

I flushed, ashamed for jumping to conclusions.

"Nineteen…hundreds?" I guessed.

"Well done. Nineteen-oh-five, England. The woman on trial is a midwife. At this time, midwifery was legal per the Midwives Act of 1902, but…"

Grandma sighed. "No, this needs to start earlier. The Bible passage about not suffering a witch to live is a gross mistranslation. Long story short—"

"Thank you," I muttered under my breath. Not quietly enough, because she shot me a look that, if there were any energy behind it, would have turned me into a frog. Or a puddle for a frog.

"As I was *saying*, women were the first health practitioners. They knew herbs and how to make poultices, things we lost for a long time. Know why toothpaste is mint-flavored?"

"Tasty?" I ventured.

"Soothes the stomach," she said.

"Like after-dinner mints." I felt proud of myself for that.

"Wafer-thin mint?" she asked in a lilting voice.

"*What?*" I said.

"Your mother…your education…" she sputtered. She waved her hands dismissively. "I'll deal with her later. My point is that women knew how mint and ginger were good for digestion, and feverfew eases headaches, and valerian is useful for pain relief…you get the idea. Thousands of years of women knowing what the eff they were doing, and then men create the field of medicine and codify it into a course of study that women aren't even *allowed* to take, and they decide that herbalism is dangerous because they don't believe in it and letting blood is oh so better, and…"

She was getting worked up. I put a hand on her arm. "Careful, Grandma. Don't give yourself a heart attack."

"I'm dead, Ember. I don't have a beating heart, technically."

"Still," I said.

"Right. Men decided that women didn't know diddly squat, and the original bit in the Bible was about poisoners, which got translated to herbalists, which got translated to witches. And here, in the early nineteen hundreds, doctors didn't like that women preferred midwives—other women who understood exactly what childbirth felt like—over their lack of bedside manner. So they decided midwifery had to be official. A woman who wanted to be a midwife had to do three months of training and notify her intention to continue practicing annually."

"And this is relevant how?" I asked. "I mean, *are* they all witches?"

"Many of them, yes," Grandma said. "Herbal knowledge comes from earth-based energy. Adding a boost of magic can't hurt when it comes to healing somebody."

I looked down at the woman on trial. "And her? Why is she on trial?"

My grandmother shook her head. "Officially? Not being a registered midwife—she tried, but her reading skills weren't enough to get her through the training. But let's be honest: doctors didn't like that midwives—registered or not—helped destitute women..."

"Got it," I said. Destitute women who couldn't afford another mouth to feed.

"Okay, so witches were persecuted," I said, feigning boredom even though my heart ached for the woman on trial. (Even though I knew she was long dead, it felt real, here, now.) "I already knew that."

My grandmother sighed again, took my hand, yanked me back through a rift into the spinning stars, then through another....

What followed was what I'd call the dreaded montage if this were a movie. Brief glimpses of a variety of cultures and places, women (and sometimes men) worshipping, healing, casting circles and drawing energy and doing things I didn't recognize except to understand it was all related.

"Paganism, Wicca, the Old Ways. Druidism," Grandma's voice echoed in my head. "In other countries, Norse mythology, Greco-Roman, Asian, what have you. It's not about a belief in a god, or multiple gods, or god-excuse explanations of the world, but the relationship with the earth, air, fire, water. The patterns of the world. Intuition. Deep knowledge."

I couldn't deny it: the words "deep knowledge" struck something deep inside of me, resonated. Maybe—okay, I would deny this out loud—brought tears to my eyes.

Then we were dropping into more recent times. My grandmother, fighting to make paganism an official religion. The success when it was recognized by the US military. Witches around the world connecting at the same time to give healing strength on Earth Day.

And then, last year.

My mother and her best friend, Kimberly, in Kimberly's kitchen, as Kimberly complained about Philippa.

"Jealousy is a negative emotion, and it'll suck away your energy if you let it continue," my mother told her.

Now in our own plant-filled sunroom, my mother with a group of her friends, and one of them, Maggie, saying to Kimberly, "Everyone has different strengths and weaknesses."

But then we were outside, pre-dawn, and my mother and Philippa were both creeping around through the snow, depositing baked delicacies and other gifts at all the houses in the neighborhood.

"The argument between Kimberly and Philippa was, in many ways, about who could give more," Grandma said. "Sure, Kimberly had always been the one to do all this, and Philippa challenged her standing in the community, and yes, things got out of hand. Nobody's perfect, especially when there's a clash of strong personalities."

I couldn't think of anything to say to that.

Another montage, showing me that Mom and the coven also delivered tins of cookies and treats to emergency rooms and fire stations and police stations every year on Christmas Eve, New Year's Eve, the Fourth of July—times when people couldn't be home with their families, when accidents and injuries were at their worst.

Those goodies, Grandma told me, were imbued with strength and hope, so that the people on the front lines could keep going.

And then there were the gifts delivered to local hospital wards.

I deny that I shed any tears then. Do not push me.

Then we had one final stop in time....

My mother, in town on a sunny autumn day, her cloth shopping bags bulging as she walked back to her car. Suddenly, she froze. Her head whipped around.

Then she dropped the groceries, ran down the sidewalk, and pulled a kid back from stepping into the road, even though no cars were visible.

The car whipped around the corner a few seconds later.

My mother and her friends *did* use their abilities to make the world a better place. Not by any grand gestures.

By one person at a time.

Message received.

I cursed in a way that would make my mother proud.

Or not.

Ember

Then we were back in my bedroom. I glanced out the window. It was still dark, still night.

"I brought you back to seconds after we left," Grandma said.

I was exhausted. I kissed Grandma on the cheek, fell onto my bed, and despite how my brain was whirling with everything I'd seen, I was out before I could even burrow under the covers.

Dana

"Good morning," I said cautiously when Ember stumbled blearily into the kitchen. I slid a heavy white mug of coffee—cream, three sugars—across the counter to her, because, of course, I'd known she was about to walk in.

Her blond curls were tangled and her pajamas looked more than slept in.

"Thanks," she said by way of greeting. She slid onto a kitchen stool, took the mug in both hands, and drank deeply.

"How are you?" I asked cautiously.

"You sicced Grandma on me," she said, lowering the mug and glaring at me. "She says she's going to have words with you about music and wafer-thin mints."

I stared at her. I hadn't expected that *at all*.

She shrugged. "I didn't get it, either."

"Did…your grandmother have anything else to say?"

She buried her face in her mug. When she reemerged, she looked more like herself. Caffeine. So magical, you'd think witches invented it.

She took a deep breath. "I'm sorry for what I said yesterday. I didn't understand everything, and I think I have a better grasp now."

"Apology accepted," I said. "I'm sorry I didn't explain enough earlier."

She nodded, and set the mug down carefully. "After I shower, I'd like to bake cookies with you." She didn't look up until the end of her sentence, as if afraid of what my reaction would be.

I tried to keep myself from full-on beaming, because I knew that would provoke at eye roll, at the very least. "I'd like that, too," I said.

"Can I invite Isla?"

"If it's all right with her mother."

She slid off the stool and hugged me. Best feeling in the world, even if she *was* taller than me.

I watched her leave the kitchen.

It was time for my little witchling to learn what she could do.

END

THE PORTLAND HEDGEWITCHES SERIES

HEDGING THE WITCH

DAYLE A.
DERMATIS
"…One of the best writers working today."
– USA Today bestselling author Dean Wesley Smith
HEDGING
THE
WITCH
A Portland Hedgewitches Short Story

ABOUT THIS STORY

An honest politician: far more rare than hedgewitches, at least in Portland, Oregon.

When one such politician asks hedgewitch sisters Holly and Willow to investigate whether his rival employs a magical advantage, Holly's familiar, Cam, must support Holly through a treacherous investigation...or risk losing her forever.

The first story in a spellbinding new urban fantasy series by the author of the Nikki Ashburne Ghosted stories.

HEDGING THE WITCH

I EASED under the front door of the magic shop, a pale grey mist indistinguishable from the tendrils that hung low on this November day of Portland, Oregon, drizzle, and reshaped, solidifying into my most common form, that of a human male.

Willow was working the front counter, which was the usual state of things. Slender as her name suggested, she wore layers of velvet against the day's chill, in claret and midnight blue, with tea-stained lace peeking from beneath her skirt and at her wrists. Her hair curled around her shoulders, streaks of pale green peeking through the light brown. Her eyes, as she looked up and smiled a greeting, were green, as befitting a hedge witch.

"She's in the back," Willow told me. "I'll close up." Also the usual state of things. Holly, her sister, could be as prickly as *her* name suggested, and was less suited to dealing with customers.

The shop—the ground floor of a purple-and-slate-blue Victorian tucked down a side street in the trendy Hawthorne District—bore no sign. Unlike the various pagan and New

Age shops in the area, it didn't cater to the casual dabbler or the tourist. Holly and Willow's shop was for true magic users.

The house had been in their family since it was built, and the sisters had maintained its Victorian accents, from the dark gingerbread in the corners of the archways between rooms to the pocket doors with their cast and burnished brass fittings. The dark wood floors creaked in places and the colored glass in the dining room built-ins had been re-leaded at least once, and the push-button light switches and lavender glass doorknobs were original.

To the sisters, the house was old. To me, not nearly as much.

Dried herbs, potions, and concoctions—Willow's talent—and Holly's amulets and charms filled glass-fronted lawyer's bookcases, along with a small number of leather-bound old grimoires. Open shelving held the usual candles, seeds, cauldrons, bells, athames, and the like. Branches dripping with dried moss hung in the corners, and pretty crystals caught the light in the windows during the summer. Now, though, Willow had a fire glowing and snapping in the fireplace flanked by brass andirons shaped like greyhounds.

The shop smelled of woodsmoke and lavender and amber, a mix of comfort and magic. Before Willow turned off the music that flowed softly from hidden speakers, I paused. I'd spent enough years in the human world to know much of its music. Florence + the Machine, if I wasn't mistaken.

I passed through the swinging door to the private area of the house. The shop consisted of the foyer, dining room, and two parlors; back here was the eat-in kitchen, sun porch for preparing herbs, and the back staircase leading to the bedrooms and work rooms.

Holly sat at the kitchen island, a broad construction with

white beadboard sides and a soapstone top, oiled regularly over the last century to give it its dark grey patina. Her short, dark brown hair was spikey and shot through with dark green. She wore skinny jeans and a sapphire-blue sweater, a silk infinity scarf in peacock co when her father was at his office in the city and the servants were busy elsewhere, lors looped around her neck. Her low-heeled, knee-high brown boots were hooked on the rugs of the barstool. She had a sandwich in one hand and her iPhone in the other, and a white cat sitting on the stool next to her.

She was my witch.

And I was her… Well.

Somewhere down the centuries, the relationship between witches and magic became twisted by the non-magical who walked the earth, who didn't understand. Familiars, as we came to be termed, were believed to be witches' servants, or even pets.

Nothing could be further from the truth.

We were spirits of the earth, of nature—what most call fae folk, or fairies (or any of the infinite spellings thereof). We could not *do* magic. We *were* magic.

Witches, on the other hand, had the innate ability to perform magic, and used our energy to do so, to channel and weave their spells.

The closest word in English I knew to define our relationship was *symbiotic*.

We each seek a witch most aligned to our energies. Generally we are bonded for the life of the witch (we fae have a longer span of existence), although any number of things could break that bond, or cause a witch and familiar to choose to part ways. Uncommon, but not impossible.

In some cases, a familiar stayed with a family. I had not, however, been connected to either of the twins' parents, nor had Willow's familiar.

Names are mutable things, for for creatures such as us, deeply private. They have power, entwined with our own power, and to share them is to literally give up a part of ourselves.

Also, our names are impossible for humans to pronounce.

So our witches give us names, names that work for them, names that will be so easy to remember in a time of crisis that it will be the only word, the last word they have.

Holly called me Cam, short for Camelot, because, she said, of my posh accent. That I wasn't offended says as much about her as it does me, and our relationship.

"Cam," she said now, her gaze flicking up from her phone long enough to acknowledge me. She tapped the phone a few times, then shut it off and set it on the island. "Just checking on some shipments."

I nodded. "I'll put the tea on," I said. After filling the electric kettle and plugging it in, I put out teacups and tapped tea into strainers atop each cup: bracing Irish Breakfast for Holly; Lady Grey, a milder cousin of Earl Grey, for Willow; Darjeeling for myself out of long habit.

"Richard's assistant will take Irish Breakfast as well," Willow said as she came through the swinging door from the shop. "For Richard..." She thought for a moment. "The spearmint with mugwort."

One of her own blends. Willow's skills were with plants: gardening, herbology, and concoctions, along with healing; her strengths were associated with earth and water, which nurtured growing plants, and the spring and summer months, prime growing seasons.

Holly's talents lay with animals, weather, air, and fire; she could read auras and had an affinity for protection spells.

The spearmint swirled in fragrant steam as I poured the water, masking the scent of the pinch of mugwort. The herbs were for fortitude and strength. Appropriate for Richard

Quillen, who was running for state senator and would be arriving at any moment.

Richard had approached Willow recently, asking for some assistance—and discretion. Witchcraft was accepted, but viewed with suspicion in certain circumstances. The political arena was one. People wanted to believe they voted with a clear head for the best candidate, not that they had been manipulated by magic. Very, very few witches could do that kind of manipulation, and none on a wide scale, but ignorance bred distrust.

Richard and Willow had dated very casually and briefly in college, and he came to her because he believed he could trust her. It was unlikely anyone could dredge up their relationship, but even so, Holly and I had agreed to assist him, because the link between Holly and Richard was much more tenuous.

The stories about familiars spying for their witches do brush against the truth of things. It is a fact that, because of our mutable shape, we can go places and observe things that witches cannot.

When everyone was assembled, I'd share what I had learned.

The perimeter of the house and yard was spelled, not so much with a compunction that people not look here, but that whatever they saw (or heard, and so forth) wasn't worth noting, much less remembering. It served us well when what we did would look to outsiders like eerie lights flashing, or sound like booming thunder.

It served Richard well, because if any reporters happened to be paying attention to him, they'd not think it worth mentioning that he came to the shop, and soon forget they'd noticed.

He was accompanied by his personal assistant, Adriana. Her straight blond hair was pulled back into a ponytail that brushed past her collar. Her tortoiseshell glasses had intricate wire openwork earpieces and a unusual shape. In Portland, "unusual" was unremarkable. She was efficient to a fault and suffered no fool, gladly or not, which meant she and Holly butted up against one another like two duelists certain that the other has caused deep offense.

We assembled in the finished basement that ran the length and width of the house. Comfortable leather sofas and chairs in distressed burgundy leather ringed a round coffee table etched with Celtic knotwork. The walls were a warm golden color, and framed photos of labyrinths from around the world hung from the picture rail. Holly and Willow lit a few fat, white candles on shelves in the corners, the warm smell of wax warring with the scents of tea and molasses cookies, which Willow had taken from the oven moments before Richard and Adriana arrived.

The twins did more powerful spells in another area, which was even more heavily warded and guarded. Another door led to the laundry room; if I listened carefully, I could hear the hum of the dryer.

Holly took a cookie and sat back, balancing her mug of tea on the arm of her chair as a grey-and-white cat jumped onto her lap and settled in. Richard and Adriana sat catty-corner, each at an end of a sofa, each sitting forward, ready for the business at hand, although Richard had taken a sip of tea.

The seat where Willow's familiar, Eoin, usually chose was painfully empty. We avoided looking at it. Something had happened to Eoin a few months ago, but Willow wouldn't speak of it. Not even to Holly, her twin and closest confidante.

We hoped she would chose to, or be able to soon.

"Your suspicions were correct," I said without preamble. "Ms. Heche has a witch in her employ, a powerful one, and one I believe is not as interested in following the rules and laws of polite magical society if his goals may be realized that way."

Marianne Heche was Richard's opponent in the senatorial race. She was smart, savvy, and an excellent orator. Twenty years older than Richard, she also had the gravitas of age and wisdom on her side.

She also, apparently, would stoop to levels Richard wouldn't.

"How does that affect us?" Adriana asked. As with fools, she had no patience for vague language. "What do we have to be prepared for?"

I shook my head. "Alas, there was no discussion of *what*. I heard no indication that Marianne or the witch meant any harm, but rather intend some sort of disruption," I said to Richard. "Perhaps something to discredit or embarrass you."

"But your upcoming fundraiser was mentioned"—I directed this to Richard—"so I suggest having some measure of magical security in place."

He put down his mug, blew out a breath. He was a handsome man in that politician way: perhaps a bit too slick, but he seemed to have good intentions. His reddish-blond hair was as expensively cut as his grey suit, and he balanced his broad-shouldered height with a voice that often tended to the soft side, just enough to make people lean in to listen more carefully.

Beyond that, and what Willow had said about him in college (smart, focused on his studies, volunteered at a legal aid clinic), I didn't know. I wasn't exactly a citizen who was registered to vote, so I had no interest in his—or Marianne Heche's—politics.

I had only my own intuition, and I believed him to have integrity.

I knew less about Marianne Heche, but I didn't respect or

trust her win-at-any-cost attitude. Especially if it involved magic that could become dangerous.

Any magic could become dangerous, even if unintentionally so. That was why there were rules.

"I see your point," Richard said. "I don't want to have magic as part of my campaign, but if it has to be a countermeasure of some sort…"

"They could be doing this to force your hand," Adriana warned. She didn't miss a trick, that one. "Make you look like you're going back on your word not to be involved with magic."

"Unless, of course, there just happened to be a witch and familiar at your fundraiser because they, oh, say, endorsed your campaign," Holly said casually. We all looked at her. "Which wouldn't be a lie," she added, and ate the last bite of her cookie.

"Adding you to the guest list," Adriana said, already tapping at her iPad. She glanced up at me, a question in her eyes.

"Cam Arthur," I said.

It was as good a last name as any.

The fundraiser was being held down in Eugene, a city about two hours south of Portland. Or, rather, it was being held in the outskirts, up in the hills, at a teaching zoo. Holding events allowed them to offer more scholarship money to needy students.

"Points to Quillen," Holly commented.

Large white tents had been erected in a central courtyard, with tall heat lamps every few yards. Had it rained heavily or the temperature plummeted, the fête could have been moved inside, but the night was clear, the stars winking in the ebony autumn sky, along with a rising crescent moon.

Richard would give his speech after supper. For now, the tents were filled with the sounds of cutlery clinking against plates and the murmur of conversation. The oaky white wine was deliciously dry.

For all we were supposed to be guests and not be official witch-and-familiar presence, our simple had turned into an operation worthy of a tactical team. Holly and I were able to communicate silently, and for short periods of time, so could she and her sister—that type of magic was draining for witches. Willow, meanwhile, was outside the zoo but nearby in case we needed her assistance. She had an earpiece matching Adriana's, so Adriana could keep her informed of anything unusual that we as guests might not be privy to.

Ahead of time, we studied the zoo map, and gave careful attention during the tour that was offered as part of the fundraiser. Adriana checked and double-checked every guest against her list, and grilled the staff—zoo, catering, everyone —to ensure every employee was accounted for.

But witches have ways of being unseen, as do, obviously, familiars.

We stayed alert for any hint of someone using magic, but if the other witch had any sense at all, he wouldn't give himself away ahead of time.

For someone who generally preferred practical clothing, Holly had agreed to let Willow help her dress appropriately for the event, and she looked stunning. She wore an evergreen velvet dress that clung to her curves and accented the highlights in her hair. It was long-sleeved in deference to the autumn chill, but dipped into a low vee at the front. She wore black shoes she referred to as retro, lower heeled and with a strap across the instep.

Better, she said, for running, in a pinch.

I wore a dark grey suit with a dove-grey silk cravat, my preference over modern ties.

My nutritional requirements are not the same as humans, but I could appreciate the tender, rare roast beef, garlic new potatoes, and pureed butternut squash soup. Holly appreciated the food even more, and I knew she reminded herself to slow down, eat with less intense focus. She loved to eat, but tended to be a bit methodical about it.

Unfortunately, we'd barely had time to do more than sample the excellent meal when Holly stiffened, her fork halfway to her lips. A moment later—quickly enough that no one else noticed, she set her fork down.

I'd felt the same thing she had: power. Someone was using magic in the area.

It's more than that, she said mentally to me, and I gave her a boost so she could include Willow. *The animals are agitated. I'll go check.*

She remembered to murmur something neutral that in polite society indicated she was going to the restroom, scraped back her chair. It caught on the hexagonal cement tiles of the courtyard, but I was already on my feet to assist her, as any gentleman would. The smile she gave me was grim.

In some ways, we'd both been hoping I'd been wrong, that nothing would happen.

And none of us had considered the animals might be in danger.

I couldn't fathom what Marianne Heche would gain by it, either.

"Excuse us," I said quietly to the other donors at our table. We hadn't spoken other than to exchange basic pleasantries, and they probably wouldn't spend too much time wondering about our departure.

Without needing to speak, we went entered the gift shop,

left open tonight in case anyone wanted to spend even more money. It had several entrances and exits, including the one from the central courtyard and one that faced the zoo exit. We wound our way through the displays of stuffed animals and tchotchkes, and went back out through the door that led to the exhibits.

Like most zoos, the animals were kept in two-part enclosures. One section was for public viewing, and the other was indoors for most animals, a place where they retreated to get away from viewers or weather, to sleep, and to be tended by zookeepers. This zoo was no different, except perhaps the fact that the private enclosures behind the public ones had more space for keepers. This allowed for multiple students to view or participate in the animal's care.

We'd had a private tour as part of the fundraising fête, including spending time in the building that connected with the inner sanctums of the big cats—lion, snow leopard, cheetah—at their feeding time. The enclosed area stank of ammonia, the roars and snarls that echoed through the room as the animals demanded their fresh meat was like nothing else. Willow, despite her magical affinity with animals, said it triggered a primal, fight-or-flight response.

Pretty much all *flight*, she'd admitted, even though her rational brain had known otherwise.

Now, we didn't bother staying in the landscaped front area. We went straight to the back. Here, plain cement walkways led to austere one-story white buildings.

It was noisier than it should have been. Some kind of monkeys were screaming, and a big cat snarled.

I could smell their agitation: excrement, sharp and powerful, assaulted me.

Holly sucked in her breath, and I saw what she saw. I channeled energy her way so she could contact Willow. *We need you ASAP.*

Almost at the same time, Adriana appeared, faster than she could have from Willow contacting her. She must have seen us leave the banquet. Her gaze followed ours, and she paled.

Because what we saw, in the glow of the light above each door to each building, was that the door was open.

Not the normal door to allow keepers and students in.

The larger door that gave keepers access to bring animals out if they needed to do something that couldn't be handled in the enclosures.

When that happened, generally the animal was sedated.

The monkey I'd heard screaming was actually a lemur, and it was in a pine tree next to its enclosure.

"We need to close the doors of any animal that hasn't escaped yet—priority on the dangerous ones," Holly said, just as Willow hurried up. Unlike her sister, she'd opted for jeans and practical boots, a lacy knitted scarf and fingerless gloves of dark gold peeking out from brown leather jacket.

"Split up," Holly continued. "Don't take any chances. Adriana, if you can get ahold of zoo staff, do it."

"No," I said. "Don't involve the staff yet, if we can help it. We don't know what this witch has planned, and we want to avoid anyone else getting hurt. We'll contact them if we need help with a particular animal, and even then, we should avoid letting them know all the enclosures were opened."

"What about security?" Adriana asked. "Aren't they seeing this?"

"The witch's using magic," Holly said, mostly keeping the withering tone out of her voice. "It's not that hard to disable or fool security cameras and alarm systems."

"Of course," Adriana said briskly. If she'd heard Holly's tone, she was choosing to take the high road. "I'll take the west corner. Keep me updated." She turned and jogged away, which was rather impressive given the height of her heels.

"Dibs on south," Willow said, and dashed off.

"I've got the lemur," I said. "Check the big cats first."

"Already on it," Holly said, and headed in that direction.

I turned and looked up into the pine. The lemur's huge golden eyes stared down at me, and it opened its mouth to scream.

I spoke one word, in the language of my people, an ancient language of the earth and air and fire and water that binds the world together.

The lemur froze. It didn't understand the word, but the meaning behind it would have been clear to any living creature. It meekly climbed down out of the tree and loped through the nearby door. I checked inside to ensure none others had escaped—lemurs were nocturnal, after all. Those were the animals we needed to worry most about, unless the other witch was also doing something to wake the diurnal animals up.

All lemurs were accounted for; I could sense them because of my connection to the earth rather than see all of them. I closed the door, which automatically locked behind me.

I checked on the rest of the primates and marsupials, and found them safe, although a koala had crept close the door and was eyeing the escape route with interest.

The zoo wasn't particularly large, just a few acres, with the habitats fairly clustered, so I would soon intersect with the others.

"Hey hey hey, not that direction—go this way. There you go."

I turned to see Willow behind a lumbering anteater, making shooing motions with her hands to direct it back to its enclosure. Then I saw the line of ants ahead of it, moving at a speed just faster than the anteater's. An illusion cast by

Willow, no doubt with the necessary scent to entice the anteater.

It was a fairly placid creature. We'd have more problems with potentially dangerous animals—perhaps that was what Marianne Heche's pet wizard had been intending?

But that still didn't make sense. Yes, it would disrupt the fundraiser, but it wouldn't be a black mark on Richard Quillen's political campaign or him personally.

I couldn't wrap my head around how this incident would backlash onto him.

Cam. Need you stat.

I sent Holly magical energy before I asked, *What's going on?*

Cranky snow leopard. Have to hitch it in.

In that case, she'd need more magic than what I'd just given her.

Holly's ability with animals included hitchhiking with them: becoming one with them and experiencing the world through their senses—and controlling them.

It was a difficult thing to do, even with the animal's consent. She always requested the animal's consent; that was one of the rules of polite magical society.

However, if the snow leopard—which had the potential to be a danger to others—was cranky, as she put it, she might find herself in a tug-of-war for control. And that would make it even crankier and less malleable.

The bond my witch and I had couldn't be severed by mortal distance, but like anything else, the connection had strength the closer we were to one another. The sooner I was with her, the better I could give her what she needed to do her magic.

I took in a deep breath, aligning myself with the mortal and immortal worlds, which were magic just as I was magic. The same magic, the same energy. Then I shifted into the form of a brown hare, fast and fleet, and made my way to Holly.

Although I shifted quickly to my natural form when I arrived, the snow leopard scented me. Its black-spotted white head swung in my direction, and a low, dangerous rumble sounded from its throat. I tensed, prepared to shift again, become a bird and fly up into the nearest maple tree, its leaves already past brilliant red to faded, half shedded on the ground and already swept away by a diligent maintenance worker.

I didn't even really need to be in human form to channel energy to Holly, but it was the most natural state, an automatic one.

Cam...

Holly was crouched on the ground at the corner of the big cat building, half-shadowed, her velvet dress pulled above her knees. The stance left her extremely vulnerable and not in a position to flee if needed, but it would be easier for her when she hitchhiked on the leopard if she was already at the same eye level. Otherwise the change in perspective would disorient her.

She also had to be physically close to the animal to hitchhike.

Ideally, she should be touching the snow leopard.

The snow leopard would be having none of that.

I fed her energy, and she drew it in, shaped it into her own, personal magic. To my eye, she took on an aura, a soft, wintergreen glow.

I wasn't privy to her conversation with the snow leopard, although I sensed her communion with it. If nothing else, it took the animal's attention away from me and back to her. It growled again, but not as loudly.

Still cranky, she told me. Likes its freedom; so many scents to explore.

Typical cat.

As if on cue, the leopard's ears pricked and it glanced west, toward the enclosure that housed the gazelles. At the same time, I noticed the wind had shifted, bringing new scents from that direction. If any of the antelopes were free, as far as the leopard was concerned, it had a good reason to be there.

Going in, Holly said, and I knew, just as she did, that she had to, now.

I saw the leopard tense, muscles bunching and rippling beneath its thick, spotted coat, and its lip draw back in a snarl, revealing an ivory fang. I saw Holly's body sway, staying in position only because unconscious brain function demanded it.

I could shift, become a predator to the leopard, but if the leopard was harmed while Holly's consciousness was within it, she could be harmed as well. If I killed it before she was free of it…

Then again, if it attacked her body, she'd be left without a vessel to return to.

I didn't want to lose her.

The leopard snarled again, but moved in the direction of the building. Its movements were jerky as it fought against Holly's control, fought to go in the direction it preferred.

I sensed how she tried to soothe it, and how it resisted.

Holly would have to not only get it into the building, but into the entrance to its own enclosure. Two doorways. I stood slowly, carefully. The leopard flicked a gaze at me.

I could alter my physical form, be something less like prey and yet not threatening, but I needed to follow the leopard inside and close the door to its enclosure, and for that, my human form was best.

Then I thought of something I hadn't considered, not in all my centuries.

I could change just part of my physical being.

I could change my scent.

But to what? I thought swiftly.

Another leopard might be considered a challenger. If I were ahead of the leopard, I could smell like prey, in the same way Willow had enticed the anteater with illusory ants. I was simply in the wrong place for that.

I needed the leopard to not feel threatened *or* attracted. I wanted it to be...

...repulsed.

I changed my scent to that of rotting meat. Took a step, then another.

The leopard shook its head, stepped away from me, towards the building. It knew rotting meat was to be avoided.

Holly clearly used this to her advantage, and encouraged the beast further.

Between the two of us, we convinced it that it was rather be in its enclosure, where fresh, safe meat was regularly provided.

As I closed the inner door, I saw the snow leopard take a hitching step, as if it had missed its footing, and knew Holly had pulled out of its mind. The leopard turned and growled, and I backed away. By the time I had the outer door closed, and heard it lock automatically, Holly was rising, smoothing her dress down.

I saw her take a hitching step of her own, and was at her side in an instant, supporting her. Hitchhiking on an animal was a strain under normal circumstances, and even more draining when the animal fought for control.

Her lip curled, not unlike the leopard's expression. "Ech. You stink."

In truth, although the night was cold, her exertion had left her perspiring, but I thought it prudent not to mention that. I hastily shifted my essence to remove the smell of decay.

She was still weak, but with my assistance was rapidly regaining her strength, enough so that she could contact her sister.

I'm done, Willow responded. A pause. *Adriana too. Coming your way.*

"Everyone accounted for?" Holly asked when they arrived.

Willow nodded, and Adriana said, "As best as I can tell from my list without having assistance from the staff. Some of the smaller animals are difficult to spot."

I wasn't surprised Adriana had a complete list of every animal at the zoo.

We headed back to the fundraising dinner. We entered the gift shop, and Willow moved to exit out the door that led away from the zoo, so she wouldn't be seen. But as Adriana reached for the handle of the door that let to the central courtyard, Holly, Willow, and I all froze as one, with Holly reaching out to stay Adriana's hand.

"More magic," she said.

Willow came back to us. "It's close," she said. "And he's spelled so people won't notice him."

"Which means he's doing something close to the dinner," I said. "Where he might be seen otherwise."

"Then how can you tell he's there?" Adriana asked.

"The spell's not set up to distract another witch," Willow explained. "Richard pledged not to use witches in his campaign, so Heche's witch assumed there aren't any witches here."

"Or he's arrogant enough to assume we won't sense his power, or we won't intervene," Holly said.

"What is he doing?" Adriana asked.

I glanced at the witches. They shook their heads. "It's not clear," I said. "We need to find out."

"We need to stop him," Holly said.

It was my turn to shake my head. "Only if he's doing something that needs stopping," I said. "Otherwise we run the risk of exposing ourselves, which could have a negative impact on Richard's campaign."

We went back out the door we'd entered.

"Watch Richard," Willow said, and slipped away. "I'll see if I can find the witch."

The three of us stepped off the path into a decorative shrub with arching eight-foot-high branches and dark green leaves that were turning orange at the edges, forming a shadowed, private canopy. It was one of many copses that ringed the courtyard, with a few breaks for cement pathways leading towards the zoo or the school buildings.

Under the white tents, the plates had been cleared, small dishes of dessert and fragrant cups of coffee and small glasses of après-dinner drinks taking their place on the white linen tablecloths.

Richard stood behind a podium, his expensive suit impeccable, his melodious voice coming through the sound system, thanking everyone for coming and for their support.

Everything looked calm. I couldn't use magic to create spells, but I could commune with the natural world, and I felt nothing out of the ordinary. No animals where they shouldn't be.

"Maybe—" Adriana whispered.

Holly raised a hand, forestalling the other woman's words. "Willow's found the witch," she said.

A moment later, an image appeared in my mind and, no doubt, Holly's. A man in dark clothing, lying prone on the ground. His arms were out in front of him, further obscuring his face, but his pale hair, so blond it looked white, bore a crimson streak. For a moment I thought it was blood.

Then Holly said aloud, in a tone dripping with disgust, "Bertram Shayne."

"You know him?" I asked, even as I saw, through Willow's eyes, the whole scene. The witch lay in a copse similar to ours, almost directly across the courtyard from us. I recognized the sturdy red alder tree as his familiar.

"Haven't seen him around much lately," Holly said. "Thought he'd left the area. He's powerful. Likes to skirt the rules. And he's a grade-A asshole."

"Former paramour of yours?"

"Shut up." She didn't waste her time glaring at me. "I'm surprised he'd get mixed up in something like this—then again, I haven't seen him in a long time. People get assholier."

"His familiar?" I asked, even though I suspected what the answer would be.

"Don't know."

The relationship between witch and familiar is not only symbiotic and close, but private. Witches don't necessarily "share" us, and we are naturally reclusive. A situation such as Holly and Willow's—sisters living in the same house—made it more likely that their familiars would know each other and the other witch, as did any family arrangement. When Willow bonded with a new familiar, we would work together when necessary.

"What's he doing?" Adriana asked, and on the heels of her question, almost before she finished asking it, Holly swore.

"Spider," she said.

Then it was Adriana's turn to curse, as she spotted and pointed to the fat, dark brown tarantula that had just begun to make its way out of the greenery behind Richard and the podium

Too small. That's why I hadn't sensed it: I hadn't been looking for a tiny thing.

"I closed all the cages at the Insects and Arachnids building, but I couldn't tell if all the bugs were there." Adriana whispered both out of the need to be quiet and, I guessed, because of the crushing knowledge that she'd failed. She didn't seem the type to accept mistakes, whether in herself or others. "I checked as carefully as I could," she said. "Some of them…hide."

If Willow were here, she'd reassure Adriana that it wasn't her fault. Unfortunately for her, she had Holly.

But I was there as well. "You weren't trained to spot them," I said. "However, we need to focus on the problem at hand. Tarantulas aren't dangerous to humans. Why is Bertram controlling it?"

"It's not about him being in danger," Adriana said. "He's terrified of spiders. Phobic."

"What'll he do if he sees it? Or if it climbs onto the podium—or him?" Holly asked.

"I imagine at the very least, he'll scream like a little girl," Adriana said. Her tone turned brisk and somewhat detached despite her words. She had pulled herself back together. "He's also likely to run away, or even faint. He'll be humiliated."

"And the press will eat it up, especially the way Heche's camp will spin it," Holly concluded.

"They will endeavor to discredit him," I said. "If a man can't handle a little shock like this, how would he be able to comport himself in a major crisis? He'll seem flighty, untrustworthy."

"We need to tell zoo staff," Adriana said, her phone already in her hand. "They'll know how to—"

"No," Holly said. "There's no time. I'll have to hitchhike on it. Control it," she added, the brief, clumsy explanation for

Adriana's benefit. "Plus staff will cause a fuss, and Richard will still see it and get flustered."

To me, she added, albeit unnecessarily, "I need a safe place."

I nodded; I'd been scanning the area since she posited the plan, one I'd been formulating at the same time. She needed somewhere where she could be unseen, but close enough to the spider to become one with it.

The plan was fraught with peril.

For one thing, small, less developed creatures such as arachnids and insects were harder to hitchhike on; their brains were more foreign than a mammal's or bird's.

For another—which by the look on her face Willow had figured out as well—it was obvious from the spider's jerky movements that it wasn't going in the direction it really wanted to. I suspected it preferred the underbrush to being out in the open, exposed to potential predators.

Which meant someone already *was* hitchhiking on the spider. The other witch.

The decorative landscaping cluster of groomed under-brush and a few trees wasn't large enough for Holly to lie prone on the ground without being seen. Bertram was casting a spell to shield himself from notice.

But Holly had a more difficult task than Bertram. She would have to remove the other witch from influencing the tarantula, or fight for control. Difficult, and potentially dangerous…and she was already tired from her work with the snow leopard.

She didn't have the ability to do that *and* hold the shielding spell.

"We need Willow," I said, quickly explaining why and giving her the energy to call her sister. "That's more impor-tant than keeping watch on Bertram. What are you doing?" I directed the question at Adriana, who was bringing her phone to her ear.

"Calling the police."

"No!" Holly and I said at the same time, and Holly grabbed Adriana's arm.

Adriana, who normally schooled her expression to a bland political neutrality, looked startled, then scowled.

"This man needs to be stopped," she said.

"He'd be given a slap on the wrist at best," I said. "Heche would have him out in a heartbeat, and the charges would likely not stick. It would be hard to prove he had anything to do with the cages being open—we're the only witnesses and he won't show up on security cameras—and the spider can be argued away as a harmless prank. It's more important to stop *that*, then worry about Bertram. The magical community is more equipped to deal with him."

As I spoke, I was keeping on eye on the tarantula's progress across the hexagonal cement tiles toward the podium. Bertram must have sensed us, because the tarantula had moved more than halfway to Richard.

Adriana reluctantly lowered her phone.

"We need a shielding spell," I said to Willow, who'd arrived as I was talking to Adriana.

To create a new shielding spell, as opposed to the ongoing one around the house, would take more magic than she could draw from the world around her. I could, to a relatively small degree, siphon her some of my magic, even though I wasn't her familiar. It should be enough to allow her to do the spell.

I would have to apportion the magic carefully. There were limits to even my source of magical energy—I could drain myself to the point where I was no longer useful to them, or even to my own detriment—and Holly needed the most, especially as tired as she already was.

Willow cast the shielding spell, and Holly stretched out on the ground, her legs extending past the greenery, heedless of her dress. Nothing to be done about that. Perhaps we should always bring a change of clothes for her.

As before, I fed her energy, saw the wintergreen shimmer around her. Her arms were stretched out before her, and her fingers flexed, mimicking spider legs.

Tarantulas were as much a part of the life of the earth as anything else, but I could understand why some found them off-putting, even frightening. Just as the tarantula instinctively feared predators, humans instinctively feared things that could harm them, too, and many varieties of spiders could be harmful to humans.

The tarantula stopped. From this distance, I couldn't see the spiny hairs that covered it, the gleaming black eyes, but I could sense its confusion as a second mind tried to shoulder its way in.

Holly moaned softly. Adriana stiffened at the sound, her eyes on Richard. I doubted he heard, but either way, he didn't pause in his speech. Didn't turn around, which would be disastrous.

Still, I was more concerned about Holly. The toes of her shoes scraped against the walkway; her fingers splayed stiff, then curled again as she fought for control.

I rarely wish for the ability to control magic, to weave spells. I am content with what I am. But at rare moments like this, I do wish I had the means to help.

All I can do is give of myself, of my essence and being, and trust Holly had the strength and skill to prevail.

We watched, tense, as the spider hesitated. As it moved forward, then back, each inch a triumph or tragedy. I felt Holly's struggle as if it were my own, knew as she drew on her last reserves as well as mine. I knew Willow felt it, too, through the bond of twins.

Slowly, a few steps at a time, the spider retreated. Holly weakened Bertram's control of the tarantula's brain, allowing the spider more autonomy to do what it really wanted to do: flee the open sky to the safety and sanctuary of the underbrush.

The creature was perhaps a foot from the greenery when it stopped. Bertram was rallying; Holly was tiring. I placed a hand against the trunk of the shrubbery that helped hide us, rallied myself, pouring magic into Holly for her to use.

A long, tense moment later, Bertram's control of the tarantula snapped, and the spider scurried into the landscaping.

Holly let out a long sigh, and dropped her head, her cheek on the dirt, her eyes closed.

"I'm sorry, but you can't rest yet," I said. "You need to get cleaned up before anyone sees you."

She muttered a few choice words under her breath, but allowed me to help her to her feet. She staggered, caught herself; planted her feet firmly and drew in a few deep breaths.

"Okay," she said finally, and I released my hold on her.

"Willow, can you assist her to the ladies' room?" I asked. "Adriana, now would be appropriate to alert zoo staff that you've spotted an errant tarantula that needs to be returned to its enclosure. I'll find Bertrand and his familiar."

With any luck, the other witch would be even more drained than Holly.

I didn't mention how drained I felt myself.

Unfortunately, by the time I got to where Bertram and his familiar had been, they were gone, with a whiff of a spell to erase any traces of their path. I sank onto a bench and closed my eyes, allowing myself a moment of recovery.

The magic of nature, of the world, was eternal, everlasting. As a fae, I was not just tied to it—I was a part of it. I would need time to rest, but I would recover.

We would give our report, and the magical community would deal with Bertram as best it saw fit. Perhaps we had made an enemy. We would deal with that when the time came.

The night was clear, but the temperature was dropping. No one would think twice about a hint of fog.

I stood, dissolved into mist, and went to join my witch.

RELEASING THE SPELL

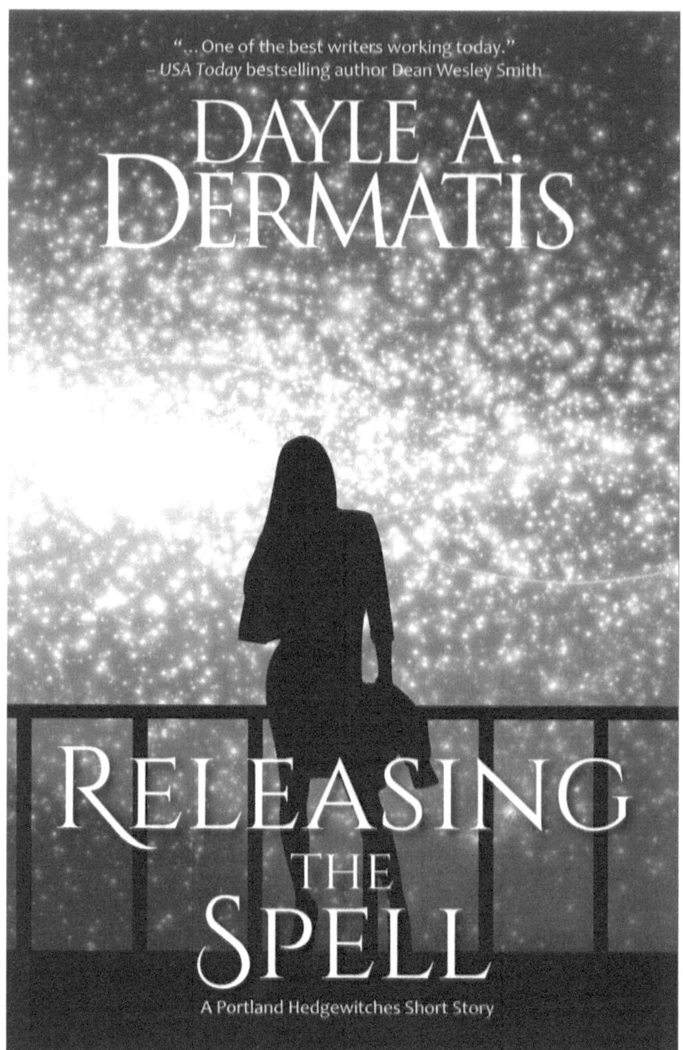
"...One of the best writers working today."
– USA Today bestselling author Dean Wesley Smith
DAYLE A. DERMATIS
RELEASING THE SPELL
A Portland Hedgewitches Short Story

ABOUT THIS STORY

If you're gonna buy a spell, go to someone legit. Bargain spells? Well, you get what you pay for...

When hapless Roberta comes to Portland hedgewitch Holly asking for help with a botched spell, Holly stumbles into the spell's trap as well. Her best bet: find the witch who created the spell. In the middle of a snowstorm.

And in the process, figure out why Roberta's boss scares her so much...

A new story in the spellbinding Hedgewitch urban fantasy series by the author of the Nikki Ashburne Ghosted stories.

RELEASING THE SPELL

I BLAMED bacon for the whole sorry mess.

Well, bacon and my sister, Willow.

It was better than blaming myself, although I was the one who had to get myself out of the mess. I couldn't risk anyone else getting caught up in it.

Normally I don't work the front of our magic shop, because (as people say in my presence, and I don't disagree with them) I don't suffer fools gladly. What they probably said behind my back (which I also didn't disagree with) was that I'm prickly, like my name: Holly.

Granted, most people who come in to the shop aren't random passersby. Portland, Oregon, has enough pagan and New Age stores to keep the casual shoppers and tourists busy, and our establishment—in a slate-blue-and-purple Victorian that Willow's and my great-great grandfather built —was tucked down a side street in the trendy Hawthorne District rather than being along the main drag.

Willow was better with people. I don't say that just to get out of working up front; in fact, we all agreed my time was better served behind the scenes, creating the bespelled amulets and charms that we sell. The potions and concoctions in glass jars and bottles were Willow's purview, along with herbs for magic work, which included cooking.

You can work some powerful sorcery creating a meal.

Including breakfast. And bacon. Bacon is kind of magical on its own.

This morning Willow said she had errands to run, and when I'd protested, she'd offered to cook breakfast in exchange for my time working the register. And because I'm helpless in the face of salty, fatty, porcine goodness, I caved.

Outside, fat, fluffy white flakes drifted down. Portland doesn't normally get much snow, but the weather witches were saying this was going to be an unusually heavy winter. Weather witches work with the elements; they can't control major storms, but they can affect small areas for a short amount of time. I had an affinity for weather magic, but I was no weather witch. I could keep the front sidewalk clean of snow, though.

Our clientele was mainly magic users. Real magic users, like weather witches and hedge witches (that would be us) and ley witches and tech witches.

Which was why, when the woman walked into the shop this morning, it raised a whole cacophony of warning bells in my head. No, I wasn't mishearing the bell over the door. These were more like whooping sirens, and a jangled feeling in my solar plexus, right where it counted. We witches trusted our gut instincts.

And my gut said this chick wasn't one of us.

She was comfortably plump in that curvy way that sits naturally on some women; she was never designed to be thin and if she tried to be, she'd make herself sick or dead. Her long, straight black hair was dotted with snowflakes that faded a moment after she walked in, and I guessed she had some percentage of East Asian in her lineage, although not enough that I could peg it more closely. It also made it hard to guess her age, but I was going for maybe five or so years older than me: mid-thirties.

The edge of a colorful tattoo, maybe a lotus blossom, peeked out of the collar of her grey sweater when she unzipped the top of her coat. She stripped off her gloves. Her nails were painted dark red, but even from here I could see her cuticles were raw.

She certainly wasn't someone who'd been here before, from the way her wide-eyed, dark gaze darted around the shop. We've kept the Victorian accents that make the house beautiful: the gleaming, dark-wood gingerbread in the archway between the foyer and living room, the burnished brass fittings in the pocket doors, the greyhound-shaped andirons in the fireplace, where a fire crackled and popped, chasing away the winter chill outside and filling the room with a comforting, smoky pine scent that was better than any incense Willow could make (and she was really good). It mixed with the odors of lavender and amber, because those permeated the very walls.

Corners dripped with dried moss or graceful branches from which dangled crystals and small bells. Old glass-fronted lawyer's bookcases were filled with leather-bound grimoires, my amulets, jars and pots of Willow's herbal concoctions, and the usual ephemera of our trade: athames, cauldrons, candles, statuary, and more.

I stepped out from behind the counter and the woman's gaze bounced over to me. Relief flooded her face, make it even more obvious that her previous expression had been one of concern, if not outright fear.

"Hi," I said, adding a smile to make my voice more pleasant (a trick I've been told works, but I have my doubts). "What can I do for you?"

"I hope you can help me," she said. "I've made a mistake—I went to the wrong person—okay, I shouldn't have tried to go cheap, but—"

"Stop," I said. It came out harsher than I intended, because I really wanted her to either say something concrete or shut up. "Sorry," I added. "Just slow down, okay? Take a deep breath. I can't help you if I don't know what you need. Start from the beginning."

I might regret that—her story could go long and rambly—but I had a feeling there were important details she might neglect to tell me otherwise.

Details are vitally important when it comes to magic. If intent isn't clear, you were going to have a big ol' mess on your hands.

Even if she wasn't a witch, she'd found us for a reason, and that reason had to do with magic somehow.

"I'm sorry," she said, and did take a deep breath. "I'm Roberta," she said. "Roberta Brown. Richard Quillen recommended you."

Oh. In that case, she *had* come to the right place. Senator Richard Quillen was an old friend of Willow's, and we'd helped him out a few months previous when he suspected the other candidate in the senatorial race illegally had a witch boosting her campaign.

He'd been right, and my familiar, Cam, and I had dealt with it, with Willow's help.

"I'm Holly," I said. "Go on."

She sucked in another breath. "I needed a protection spell, but I guess I got scammed, and something's gone wrong. I didn't think I could afford…well, I like a bargain as much as the next gal, you know?"

"And you got what you paid for," I finished.

She nodded, biting her lip, and oh sweet Goddess protect me, tears started to well up in her eyes. Why wasn't Willow back yet? She was so much better at this. When someone cried, I wanted to either throw things and shout at them, or run away.

The bacon had been spectacular, but it wasn't enough to make up for a weeping customer.

"Keep talking," I said, opening the herb cabinet. Wooden canisters were arranged inside. I knew our stock well enough that I barely had to look before my hand was on the clary sage. Good for revealing truth, clary sage was. It was a first thing to try in order to reveal information about the botched spell Roberta was claiming she'd received.

"My boss at work," she said. "He's been doing some shady stuff, and now he's asked me to do something illegal. He hasn't come out and said it, but if I don't do what he asks, he'll fire me, and my rent just went up and my dog had to have surgery and I can't afford to lose my job right now...."

Portland rents *were* skyrocketing; this was not news. I waved my hand in a circle, encouraging her to get to the point. Using the small wooden scoop in the clary sage canister, I transferred some of the herb to a green Connemara marble mortar. Willow would have been better to do this, but I could handle the basics.

"I don't trust him," Roberta said. "He's always been creepy. This is the last straw. So I wanted to get a protection spell for my office, you know? To protect my job, protect me while I was in there."

"Okay, that makes sense," I said, crumbling in a rowan leaf. I gave her the benefit of the doubt that she couldn't report him without getting in trouble herself, or she didn't have enough proof, or whatever. Magic should never be the first choice to fix a problem, but there was a point when nothing else was going to work...

At least she'd come to the right place this time. Protection spells were one of my fortes, along with reading auras.

Which made me realize I couldn't see hers. I hadn't really been trying, though, so that didn't mean much.

She sniffled. I grabbed a box of tissues from behind the counter and headed over to where she stood in the archway between the living room and dining room of the house (now both being used as retail space). The pocket doors were tucked into their slots on either side, leaving a wide opening that made the rooms feel like one space. I needed a pinch of peat moss, which was stored next to the fireplace, so I might as well toss her the box on my way by.

"So is the spell not doing the job?" I asked. "Or is it doing the wrong thing?" I had mental pictures of it frying her computer—or frying her boss when he tried to enter her office.

I hadn't check the news this morning—I'd been too distracted by bacon—so I wouldn't know if there had been any suspicious deaths.

"It's working too well," she said, and a fresh wave of tears threatened to spill over. Dammit. "Nobody can—"

I took another step, and heard and felt a very faint *pop*. Like a soap bubble popping—you can't really *hear* hear it, but you know it has to have made a sound, and you believe you felt the release even if all you end up with is a slick spot on your skin and the sweet smell of soap tickling your nose for a moment.

Roberta's watery eyes widened. "How did you...? Nobody's been able to—"

I swore, and then swore again, much more harshly than I ought to in front of a client, but these were special circumstances, and I thought I was warranted, and nobody was around to tell me differently anyway.

Because right now I felt really stupid, and I hate feeling stupid even more than I hate people crying in my general vicinity.

"The spell didn't protect your office," I said. It wasn't a question; it was just me feeling the need to state the now-obvious. "It protected *you*."

And I handed her the box of tissues, because off she went again.

The spell had created a protection bubble around her, which would have been great if she were in danger of being physically or psychically attacked. This spell just wasn't what she'd wanted.

She blew her nose. "Yes," she said. "That's the problem. But nobody has been able to get through it except you. And my dog. Although that wouldn't have been so bad, really."

Mm-hmm. I didn't need the clary sage. The dog got in because the dog made her feel safe—and she'd come to me for help, and trusted me, so I got in too. Yippee. "The spell wasn't specified to your office, so it latched on to you, because you felt you needed protection. And it's too strong—whomever made this didn't focus it properly. Their attention to detail sucks. It shouldn't keep everyone out, just anyone who intends to cause you harm."

She nodded. At least she'd stopped with the waterworks. "Can you get it off me?"

"Maybe," I said. "Let me get some tools."

And that was when I encountered the real problem.

Everyone else couldn't get through the protection bubble to Roberta.

I couldn't get out.

It was like pushing against a soap bubble that wouldn't pop. The invisible barrier was gossamer thin and stretchy, like a spider web; it would bend so far before it snapped back into shape, tugging me back with it.

That was all I had time to realize before the door to the kitchen opened. Only the front rooms were part of the store; clients came back to the kitchen or down to the finished (and extra-well-warded) basement only if they needed private consultation. The open door released a fresh wave of bacon smell. Breakfast had been barely an hour ago, but my stomach reacted by begging, like Oliver, for more, please, in a low grumble.

Dammit. Now was not the time to be thinking about crispy pork goodness.

It was my familiar, Cam, and he looked worried. He'd felt the magic when I entered the protection bubble.

"Stop!" My hand shot out, palm up, in the universal Come No Closer signal. I didn't put any magic behind it, because I didn't want to hurt Cam.

And I wasn't sure if I even could.

For some reason, the story of what a familiar is to a witch got mutated and morphed by the non-magical, like a legendary game of telephone, down through the ages. Now people think familiars are magical animal companions, or animal-shaped spirits, or something along those lines. Sure, Cam could shift into any type of creature he chose, as well as become mist, water, a tree, a rock…you name it, Cam can become it.

Because Cam *is* magic. He's one of the fae folk, and that's what witches' familiars are. We can do magic, but the Fae folk can't. They're aligned with the earth, with nature—they're simply pure magic, and we tap that magical essence to help weave and create our spells.

It's a symbiotic relationship, not a master/servant one like the stories of witches and familiars that ordinary people believe. We're partners, equals. Each witch connects with a fae whose magical essence closely dovetails with his or her personal energy, and for lack of a better way to phrase it, we bond for life—although the fae live longer than humans, and can have multiple such relationships throughout their existence. There are a few things that can break the bond, but they're rare. In fact, some familiars stay within a family, although that wasn't the case with Cam.

So no, I didn't even put up a ward or barrier up to stop Cam, or a freeze spell, because it was unlikely to even work on him.

But he was smart enough to stop when I told him to. He froze in place like a regal hound, majestic and still, but coiled to spring when necessary.

He wore dark grey trousers and a slim-fitting sweater Willow had knitted for him, Celtic knotwork in variegated, watercolor shades of grey and Prussian blue and dark gold. He was tall and slender, but there was a steely core strength to him. His hair was the color of goldenrod, his eyes were stormy blue, and his cheekbones wouldn't cut just glass, but diamonds.

A fae's true name is private, and can change, and is a part of them in a way human names simply aren't. Even though Cam's power was entwined with mine, for him to share his true name with me would be to give up a deep part of himself. Fae didn't do that, and witches didn't ask them to.

Also, their names are impossible for humans to pronounce.

So I called him Cam, short for Camelot, because he has this posh accent that sounds la-di-dah upper-crust British. Because he puts up with me, he's not even offended. In fact, when he had to tell someone his full name recently, he went with Cam Arthur.

"Protection bubble," I said. "A sloppily created one, which attached to her"—I pointed to Roberta—"rather than her office like she wanted. I'm stuck inside, so don't come any closer because I don't want you to get stuck, too."

His nostrils flared. "I think such a thing would not have the same effect on me."

"Maybe, maybe not. I don't want to take the chance." For

all I knew, it could have a worse effect on him. "I didn't expect it to have this effect on me, either. It kept everyone out except me, and I don't know why." Maybe because I'm a witch? Or because Roberta felt the opposite of threatened by me, because she believed I could help her?

I felt around the edges of the bubble. It was large enough that Roberta and I could be no more than a couple yards apart—I'd been a little closer than that when I'd accidentally walked into it. It was an arm's length above our heads, and seemed to sink into the floor, but I had the sense it continued to enclose us. I moved closer to Roberta and reached out to touch the edge of the pocket door. I could feel it, but I could also feel the gossamer-thin bubble between it and my hand.

"We should call Willow," Cam said.

I pulled my phone out of the back pocket of my skinny jeans, hit the screen to dial her number. Nothing happened. "Doesn't work in here," I said. I closed my eyes, drew a little energy from Cam, and sent a mental message to Willow. Witches can project thoughts to one another across distances, have brief conversations, but like any difficult or prolonged spells, it drains us, and our familiars have only so much energy to give us—they're not a bottomless source. On the other hand, Cam and I could communicate that way with each other without either of us expending much effort.

Unfortunately, I couldn't connect with Willow that way, either. I could sense her, but either I wasn't sending well enough for her to receive, or she wasn't receptive to answering. It wasn't an efficient method of communicating, and I didn't want to drain Cam unnecessarily.

"Heads up," I said to Cam, and tossed my phone at him. It sailed through the bubble without being affected, and he caught it gracefully.

Okay, that was good to know. I continued exploring the

bubble while Roberta, silent for once, chewed on her lower lip, which I could see now was chapped.

A moment later, Cam spoke into the phone, then said, "Straight to voicemail, I'm afraid," and tossed the phone back at me.

It sailed through, although my catch was a little fumbly. (I didn't drop the phone, so I called it a win.)

Even better. I'd hate to think we were trapped in here without food. I wasn't sure how bathroom access would work, but we would find out soon enough. At worst, I had to hope Roberta didn't have a shy bladder.

"Was the spell attached to an object?" I asked Roberta. "Something you were supposed to place in your office?" With any luck, it was a stone or crystal, something that fit in her pocket—if she was carrying a purse, it was small and swathed beneath her coat.

She shook her head. "No," she said. "I sort of expected it to be, because we weren't in my office when the guy—the witch—cast the spell."

I cursed again. "Amateurs," I muttered. Time for Plan B. Well, time to figure out a Plan B. "So here's what we know," I said. "I can't do certain magic in here, although Cam and I can sense each other. I can't leave, and obviously neither can Roberta."

"Can your sister do anything?" Roberta asked. "Richard said you were both witches."

"If we can track her down, she can certainly help," I said. "But the witch who created the spell is our best bet. A witch who casts a spell can most easily dismantle it; it's a lot harder for a witch to unravel another witch's spell. Who did this?"

She look abashed. I hadn't even known what that meant until she did it. "I don't have a name. We met in the parking lot next to the Market of Choice in West Linn."

I tried not to roll my eyes too hard. "So no office or shop. Convenient. Then how did you find this witch?"

"A co-worker gave me the information," she said. "But our office is closed today because of the weather. I don't know her home number."

Cam moved to the laptop on the counter—a repurposed bookcase built-in that had been shamefully removed from another Victorian house when some damnable flipper had decided to make the place "open concept"—and looked up the co-worker, who had a disgustingly common name. We didn't have time to call each one, if their number was even coming up in his search.

New idea: we'd drive down to West Linn, a city that was essentially a suburb to the south of Portland, and see if we could pick up any traces of the witch in the grocery story parking lot.

First, though, we determined that I could close the bathroom door and have privacy, as could Roberta. Thank the gods.

I drove Roberta's car, because she was nervous about driving in snow. It was coming down harder, and getting colder; it would be below freezing tonight, which would make the roads icy. Made me grateful for the protection bubble, actually. The snow-clearing infrastructure in the various Portland-area counties was shaky; normally we didn't get enough snow to warrant a fleet of plows, and Portland was anti-salt. If we didn't solve this soon, we might be further hampered. I had some minor affinity for weather work, but I was no weather witch, and that wasn't an efficient use of my energy right now, either.

Cam made his way south by other, fae means, and we met him there.

Even though it was late morning, the parking lot was mostly deserted and a sign in the grocery's window said it would be closing at noon due to the weather. I could see the tracks on the pavement where the last car through had driven, and there was already a dusting of snow over them. The store was located behind a strip mall with the usual Starbucks, salon, a backyard bird shop, a couple of restaurants, and a UPS store. Across the parking lot was the local Post Office, and the grocery store itself backed up against woods that led down to the Willamette River.

My boots crunched in the snow as I got out of the car. I couldn't go too far before Roberta walked around to my side; the bubble wouldn't allow it. This wasn't just starting to get annoying. She'd also apologized on the way here for the mess. Repeatedly.

She was able to describe the other witch: medium height and build; brown hair from what she could see because he'd had on a knit cap; wearing a navy blue Columbia Gear winter coat, jeans, and lace-up winter boots. So, like almost every other male in the Pacific Northwest. A smattering of acne on his long face. Young—she'd been surprised at his age, said he looked barely out of high school. That didn't surprise me; although we have our abilities from birth, we have to go through a lot of training to be able to use them effectively and, more importantly, safely.

Witchcraft was generally accepted in the world, but it made a lot of people nervous, too, and for good reason. The magical community had rules and regulations, and requirements for training. But even if this kid had gotten proper training, it didn't mean he had the smarts or the savvy to do proper spells.

It didn't surprise me that he'd screw up something as relatively simple as a protection spell. Flaky kids and their lack of detail and intent. Gave us all a bad name.

So why had Roberta's co-worker recommended him? I supposed the kid could have been the only witch her co-worker knew. When I'd asked her, she shrugged and said, "I don't know. She just said he was really reasonable."

I.E., cheap. There were some things you shouldn't bargain-hunt for. Avoid two-eyes-for-the-price-of-one Lasik deals, and never skimp on spells for hire.

I stood in the middle of the small parking lot, hands on my hips, and looked around. Four cars, including ours. Another crept by on the road between the grocery store and the strip mall, then turned left to go up to the main road through town. It fishtailed a little up the hill, but managed to not spin out. Good, because the last thing we needed was a tow truck or emergency services clogging things up.

I pulled a little energy from Cam, and spread out my hands in front of me, fingers wide, palms toward the ground, feeling for an energy signal, any residue of magic. Roberta had met up with this guy at 2 a.m. today, and only discovered the spell had put the bubble around *her* when she took the dog for a walk at 7:30 a.m. before she'd heard her office was closed, and a neighbor shoveling his sidewalk rebounded off of the bubble right onto his ass.

Anyway, since the magic work had been recent, I might be able to pick up a trace, some hint to—

Oh. Geez. The kid had spewed magic everywhere. His poor familiar must be drained.

(Roberta hadn't seen the kid's familiar, which didn't mean anything. Familiars are solitary and private. The familiar could have been a mouse in the kid's pocket, or that bush over there. I squinted at the bush just to be sure. Nope, just a bush.)

Or he could be young enough to not yet have a familiar, which meant he was overtaxing himself.

"Cam, are you getting this?" I asked.

"I am," he said. "This witch doesn't have terribly good control over his magic."

"He's young, sloppy, and possibly untrained," I said. "Question is, who is he, and where is he?"

I spread my hands out again, intending to look for a trail leading away from the parking lot—the kid or his familiar could have leaked all the way home—when a car turned down from the main road, lost traction in the snow on the hill, and started sliding fast, faster than I would have expected, right at us.

Normally a car entering the grocery store's parking lot had to ease right to go around a decorative median, placed there to make you slow down when entering or exiting the lot. The driver of this car couldn't have that kind of control; the car tires weren't gripping the road. Cam ran toward the Post Office; Roberta and I thankfully were of one mind and both ran towards the store—if she and I run in opposite directions, the protection bubble would have protested, and gods know what would have happened then.

Because somehow, the car *did* turn towards us.

Then Roberta slipped in the snow and fell to her knees, and I rebounded off the inside of the protection bubble, because it stopped moving forward when she did.

I didn't have time to throw up a ward or a wall.

The car was going to hit—

The car rebounded off the protection bubble, then *disappeared.*

Da fuq?

I bent over, hands on my thighs, gasping for breath, my heart pounding. Once I had myself under control, I held out a hand to Roberta, who struggled to her feet. She rubbed her knee.

Cam raced us, graceful, the slippery snow covering not bothering him in the least.

"Are you all right?" he asked at the same time that I said, "What the hell *was* that?"

We stared at each other for a moment, and then he apparently decided that my question was more important (he was right), because he said, "Another spell, obviously. I think it was an automatic one, set to go off if Roberta came back with another witch."

"No," I said. I know I just asked what the hell had happened, but sometimes in a crisis you just blurt something out before you've thought it through. I held out my hands once again. "He was here," I said. "I can feel his magical signature."

I turned slowly and looked down the narrow street between the grocery store and the back of the strip mall, and pointed. "He was just there. Go!"

I made Roberta drive so I could focus on tracking the sparkly (invisibly speaking) trail. She shifted up too quickly and we fishtailed our way out of the parking lot, and I hoped the protection bubble could handle keeping us from getting crushed inside a crumpled metal ball. The narrow street angled right and took us up to a light at the main road.

"Turn left," I said. "And don't stop! We'll just slide backwards."

"But the light's red," she said.

Oh, those lawful good people. "There isn't a car for miles. Do it."

She did. The roads were getting really slick, but thankfully we didn't have far to go. We were on a four-lane highway heading southeast toward a bend in the Willamette River, where it curved from flowing southeast to southwest. Snow obscured the traffic lines on the pavement, and even though it was still morning, the world felt grey like a late winter afternoon. Roberta leaned forwards as if that would help her see better. I'd automatically done the same thing, so I couldn't fault her.

The highway led us to an old, narrow two-lane bridge

over the Willamette. Like many bridges in the Pacific Northwest, it had been built in the 1920s, and had pretty cement obelisks carved with an Art Deco design. Not that we had time to admire it. A car was skewed diagonal, blocking access to the bridge. It was the same car as the fake ghostlike one that had looked like it was going to hit us.

Roberta tried to ease to the side of the road, gave up, and just stopped the car. It slid a few inches, but thankfully we weren't on a hill.

I threw open my door. "Come on." I wasn't going to be able to run without her close by.

The kid was in the middle of the bridge.

Cam materialized next to us, closer to the other side of the bridge so he didn't get sucked into the bubble.

It was more jogging than running, given how slick the road was. Okay, more walking fast than jogging. Okay, like waddling like a penguin.

"Stop," Roberta shouted at the kid. "It's me, remember me? The spell I bought from you—it isn't work right. I need help."

The kid turned at her first shout, and even at this distance I saw the whites of his eyes as he jerked like a startled horse. Of course, that meant he slipped, went down hard. He scrambled to his feet, watching us as we penguin-waddled towards him.

He didn't try to cast a spell, which didn't surprise me. He'd spewed so much magic all over the parking lot last night that I was surprised he'd had any left for the fake car accident just now. Damn kids and their energy.

He glanced toward the Oregon City side of the bridge, calculated that he wasn't going to make it before we caught him. He grabbed the waist-high cement railing, already mounded with snow, and hauled one leg over.

I swore. Roberta cried, "Wait, no, don't! I'm not mad. I

don't even want my money back. I just want the spell taken away, or reversed, or whatever you call it."

The kid weighed his options and chose the stupidest one. He dropped out of sight.

Fact: the kid was our best chance of getting the protection spell reversed. Oh, there were other ways, but they might get time consuming, and I had a life. Roberta probably had a life, too. These lives didn't involve being in each other's pockets. For one thing, she talked a lot. For another, I snored.

Fact: the kid disappearing would suck, but the kid dying would suck harder.

Conclusion: go after the kid. I stripped out of my coat, yanked off my boots.

"Holly, wait!" Cam yelled.

Cam never yelled, which meant this was serious.

"It's okay—I'm protected!" I shouted back, and jumped.

I heard a scream. I'd sort of forgotten Roberta had to come with me whether she wanted to or not. I had time to feel bad about that, and then we hit the river.

I'd had time to twist around and enter the water feet-first, as straight and vertical as I could to minimize the impact. I hoped Roberta had, too, or that the protection bubble had helped her.

I was sure the kid wasn't trying to commit suicide; he'd been trying to get away from us. But the river had a strong current, and the water was cold—really, really cold.

I didn't feel the iciness directly, thanks to the protection bubble. I sensed it, but in the way you know it's cold out when you're standing by a window looking out at the snow.

Oh, I was wet, sure, but my bodily functions weren't rapidly shutting off because I'd just plunged into a frigid river without thinking it through. I did wonder if the protection bubble would keep me from drowning by allowing me to breathe underwater, but I decided I didn't want to take the chance by experimenting.

So I swam as hard as I could towards the kid, my clothes creating a lot of drag but no more than the kid's clothes were, and I didn't think he'd had the foresight to cast a protection spell for himself. Thankfully, Roberta had the presence of mind to do the same, even though she still had her coat and boots on, which was slowing her down.

The river didn't move fast here, but there was a definite pull. The kid was swimming diagonally, headed for the shore on the West Linn side.

I could sense Cam somewhere nearby. He'd become water. If I'd stopped to think, back there on the bridge, I would've realized he should've gone after the kid, not me. Oh well, in for a penny and all that. I closed my eyes for a second, reached for him, reached for his magic.

Used it to boost Roberta, and boost me. The protection bubble sort of leapt forward, closing the final distance between us and the kid.

I heard that inaudible *pop* again, as the bubble sucked the kid in.

Dammit. Hadn't thought that through, either. It was getting annoyingly crowded in here.

I took a little more magic from Cam—I didn't want to overtax him, not when I wasn't sure what else I'd need to do in the near future—but we had to get to shore before we were washed downriver to whatever was downriver. My knowledge of Portland suburbia got spotty the further south I went. I knew there were falls just above us; I didn't know if there were any below. That was an adventure I didn't need right now. There wasn't enough bacon in the world for that.

We crawled onto the bank below a stately old house, big and white. Up the slope, between the pines, I saw a sign that proclaimed it the Historic McLean House.

Cam was nearby, safely out of range of the bubble. He looked annoyed and relieved at the same time. I smiled and waved, which made him frown as he tossed me my coat and shoes. I had no idea how he'd managed to bring them along. Fae and their magicalness. I'd ask him later.

I cast a spell to dry off Roberta, the kid, and myself. I wasn't just being nice: I was invested in none of us dying of exposure, protection bubble or not. I also put a layer of warmth beneath us, since we were sitting in snow. My own limbs were rubbery from the strain of swimming and I had no desire to get up anytime soon.

The kid, however, scrambled to his feet and tried to run. I sat and smiled, bemused, as he rebounded off the bubble's interior.

"Hoisted by your own petard," I commented when he fell on his ass.

He stared at me, acne red and stark against his nearly white skin. Even though he was dry now, he'd gotten colder in the river than we had. "What?" He sounded terrified.

Well, good. He was some unlicensed boob who shouldn't be doling out spells, protection or otherwise, willy-nilly, and he'd pissed me off.

"It means you're stuck in here too, sunshine," I said. "So remove the protection spell."

He looked at Roberta. It was, after all, the spell she'd requested and paid for. Well, sort of.

She was almost as pale as he was. Last night she'd been scared enough of her boss to get a protection spell, and today she'd been flung off a bridge into the Willamette. She had every right to feel a little off-kilter.

"Yes, I want you to remove the spell," she said. "For crying out loud, I asked you to protect my *office*, asked to be protected while I was *in* my office. I didn't pay you for *this*."

She flailed a hand around to indicate the protection bubble. "I don't even want my money back. I just want this *gone*."

He swallowed hard, his Adam's apple bobbing in his skinny neck. "Okay," he said. His voice was deeper than I would have expected. "I'm just really tapped out right now…"

"Do you have a familiar?" I asked.

He looked down and shook his head. "She left. Said I wasn't ready."

I winced. Okay, that sucked. A witch's relationship with a familiar was closer and more personal than a marriage, and the breakup, while rare, could be devastating. I hoped the kid's familiar would come back when he *was* ready; there was a chance of that. Then I realized I was feeling sympathetic towards them, and got all pissed off again.

Can you pass some of my magical energy to him? Cam asked me without speaking.

Maybe, I answered. *I couldn't connect with Willow, but he's inside the bubble with me.*

To the kid, I said, "I might be able to transfer some to you. Hold out your hands."

He did, and I reached for Cam, and he for me, and I felt the magic flow into me. Not too much, so he didn't get drained, but enough to give the kid a start.

"What's your name?" I asked the kid, because I was tired of thinking of him as *the kid*, and because even human names have a certain power.

"J-Jayden."

I formed the pure magic into a ball in my hands, about the size of a cantaloupe. To us, it glowed a silver-shot green. I wasn't sure if Roberta could see it at all. I reached out and handed it to Jayden, intending to set it in his outstretched palms. "Here you go."

He took the ball of magic, and it promptly popped, scattering all over the ground between us as if a unicorn had barfed glitter.

I sat back on my heels and swore. "The bubble is dicking with my abilities," I said.

"What does that mean?" Roberta asked. "Is this this stuck on me—around us—forever?" Her voice quavered, and I had no tissues on me, and even if I did, they would've been soaked and then dried and probably wouldn't work so well now.

"It means we have to wait until Jayden here recharges," I said.

Now *he* looked like he was on the verge of tears. So help me, if they both started crying, I was going to claw my way out of here no matter what it took.

"I think I've broken something," he said. "I don't even feel like I'm recharging, and every time I try to draw energy from the earth, it hurts."

I looked helplessly at Cam.

"It's possible he's injured himself magically," Cam said. "He most likely overtaxed himself when he threw the car at us."

"It wasn't going to hurt you," Jayden protested. "It was just to make you go away."

I tossed my phone to Cam so he could try Willow again, but the call again went straight to voicemail.

There were any number of other witches I could call. Breaking the spell would take time, but it could be done. How much time was hard to say. Whether I'd murder either of my companions was up for grabs.

(It wasn't, not really. I wouldn't harm anyone except in defense, and then as little as possible to make them stop. But the desire to make them go away was very, very strong.)

"There's always Mr. Mankell," Jayden said.

"Who?" I asked.

"My boss," Roberta said. Her brow furrowed. "How do you know him?"

I fought the urge to wrap my fingers around Jayden's neck. "He's in on this, isn't he? He and Roberta's co-worker. Hiring you was part of the plan."

Jayden sagged. No matter how scared he was of Mr. Mankell, he was more scared of me right now. And so the truth came out.

When Mr. Mankell couldn't get Roberta to rig the contract bid, he hired Jayden. Near as we could piece together he bribed Roberta's co-worker to suggest a protection spell to Roberta and to recommend Jayden. He'd then also hired Jayden for a spell to allow him access to Roberta's office. The protection spell was thus supposed to protect Mankell when he was in her office, so he could use her computer and not have that activity traced back to him.

Now Roberta looked like she wanted to throttle Jayden. "You took both our money?"

"It was a job," he protested.

Not just an unlicensed boob doling out spells willy-nilly. Oh, the magical community watchdogs were going to hear *all* about him.

"So Mankell's counter-charm might weaken the bubble enough for me to get out it and really be able to do magic," I said. "It's our best bet right now."

My phone rang. Cam still had it, so he answered.

It was Willow. She'd just gotten back to the shop, and what did we need?

We needed a plan. And one was forming in my head.

A few things in our favor: Roberta had tire chains in her car, meaning we could get through the icy packed snow on the roads a little easier. I was able to use my affinity for weather magic to stop the snow along our route, so visibility was clear and it wasn't piling up more than it already had. Roberta's office wasn't too far from the magic shop, so Willow could meet us there without too much trouble.

And Roberta was able to call her boss and convince him she was willing to do what he asked and rig the contract bid, but she wanted to do it today while nobody else was in the office, because she wanted to get it over with. The greedy bastard agreed.

We timed it so we got to the office first. Roberta's company had the whole of the third floor of a 1930s office building. The interior was modern, with a cubicle farm in the center and glassed-in offices around the perimeter, industrial blue carpeting with a faint pattern of dark red and grey, and fluorescent lights—although the lights were off except for the emergency lights near the exits. The place smelled of lemon cleaner and stale coffee.

We made our way through the dimness to Roberta's office. It was small, but at least it had a window. On the blond-wood credenza behind her desk were framed photos of her dog and a three kids (her niece and nephews, she told us). There was also one of a group of people next to a couple of trophies. I couldn't help looking closer. Well, well, well, Roberta was on one of the Dragon Boat teams that raced on the river in the summer, a popular sport in the area. From the trophies, it looked as though they were a winning team. Good for her.

Thankfully Willow arrived before Mankell did. She headed straight to me for a hug, but I managed to warn her off before she was trapped in the bubble.

Her long, curly, light brown hair was streaked with pale green, a contrast to my short, spiky dark hair with its dark green highlights. Her winter coat was dark red wool with big brass buttons; a flowered scarf peeked out at her throat. She wafted the scent of roses.

"Where have you been?" I demanded.

She pressed her lips together, glanced away. "Personal business."

I winced. I'd been so wrapped up in my own problems that I'd never really considered what she might have been doing. Her familiar, Eoin, had disappeared nearly six months ago. She wouldn't speak of it, not even to me. No matter what our differences, we were twins, and had always had each other's backs. For her not to confide in me meant something was really wrong.

Roberta stood in the doorway to her office. Jayden and I had to crouch down beneath the solid half of the wall so we wouldn't be seen immediately. Willow went around the corner, into one of the cubicles.

Then we waited. My biggest fear was that Mankell had another witch in his employ, one more competent than Jayden. He might've wanted to try coercing Roberta rather than bringing out the big guns. But because Roberta had said she was acquiescing, I hoped he was assuming he didn't need backup.

At least that wish came true. He arrived alone with the stride of someone confident, cocky. I couldn't see him from my vantage point—or lack thereof, really—but Cam, invisible nearby, projected the image in my mind.

Mankell was tall, rangy, with strong features in a pale brown face, and wore a tailored suit even just to come in to work on a snow day to shake down an underling. He was probably Roberta's age, mid-thirties. He looked the type to have made it a personal goal to make his first million before he hit thirty, and now he wasn't looking back.

He smiled when he saw Roberta, and I understood exactly

why she'd never trusted him, why she'd felt she'd needed protection from him even before this.

He meant it to be a reassuring smile, but it was all predatory, all the time. Toothy, like a shark.

"Roberta," he said. "I knew you'd come around. Don't you worry about a thing. I'll make sure you're well compensated."

My ass.

"Come on in." Roberta sounded resigned. I was the tiniest bit impressed that she was playing the part so well. "I already have the bid up on my computer."

And a moment later, there was that inaudible *pop*, and Roberta stepped back into her office, followed by Mankell who was solidly *in* the protection bubble.

A part of me wanted to leap up and shout, "Caught you now!"

A bigger part of my wanted to knee him in the balls.

I settled for standing up, crossing my arms over my chest, and scowling. Jayden, at my side, also stood, but he probably didn't look menacing. Willow and Cam moved to stand outside the office, still safely outside the bubble. Willow was moving her hands, her brow furrowed, trying to to unravel the protection spell, to be at least prepared to help even if she couldn't undo it by herself. Without Eoin, she was using only the magical energy she could personally pull from the earth

"What the hell is all this?" Mankell demanded. "Roberta, whatever you're planning, it won't work. There's no proof I've done anything wrong, and these witches aren't witnesses to anything."

I raised a shoulder. "We've got Jayden here to swear you hired him, and that you tricked Roberta into hire him to get a protection spell on her office."

"Which could be argued was so she could do something illegal without being caught," Mankell said.

"Doesn't explain how you knew she would do that, and

thus you got a counterspell so you could get into her protection spell," I said. "A spell that went completely wrong, thanks to Jayden's incompetence."

"Hey!" Jayden protested, but it was a weak protest. He knew I was right.

"My word against his," Mankell said. "What counterspell?"

Jayden snapped his fingers and held out his hand. A smooth, polished disk of wood, about the size of a silver dollar and carved with symbols on both sides, floated out of Mankell's breast pocket.

"Tricks," Mankell said. "You could have planted—"

"Oh, give it a rest," I said. I plucked the wood out of the air, tossed it to Willow, who caught it easily.

"Oh, yes, simple," she said after a moment, and held it out in one hand while holding her other hand, palm out, on the edge of the bubble. I held my breath, certain her hand would go through and she'd get sucked in and we'd be in a worse mess. But she was good, very good. Her fingers curved perfectly along the curve of the bubble, and I saw the gold-green spark of her energy spread out in lines along the bubble.

There was one final *pop* and the bubble burst.

I brushed the arms of my coat, feeling as if there was magic residue, like soap bubble slime, on me. There might have been.

"You may not have broken any laws other than threatening your employee, which would be hard to prove," I said to Mankell, "but the word of three witches and a familiar will go a long way with the magical community, whose job it is to police these things. You did hire Jayden, and you did conspire to make Roberta hire him, too." I pointed at the disk of wood Willow still held. "Your essence is all over that, and that's something that can't be faked, because the spell was tied to you with your knowledge, agreement, and participation."

"Plus I have this," Roberta said, and held up her phone, which was still recording everything we'd said.

The color drained from Mankell's face as he finally realized he was in deep, deep doo-doo, and I felt better than I'd felt all day.

Even better when I'd been eating that crispy, fatty, bacony goodness for breakfast.

A breakfast that had been a long time ago. I hoped a restaurant was open nearby, despite the snow, because I was absolutely starving. Someplace with takeout, so I could eat it alone, in peace.

TELLING THE BEES

"...One of the best writers working today."
– USA Today bestselling author Dean Wesley Smith
DAYLE A. DERMATIS
TELLING
THE
BEES
A Portland Hedgewitches Short Story

ABOUT THIS STORY

Some kind of weird Sleeping Beauty curse has hit a Portland, Oregon, suburb.

Sounds like a case for Hedgewitch sisters Holly and Willow, and Holly's fae familiar, Cam.

But "weird" doesn't begin to describe what's really happening....

A new story in the spellbinding Hedgewitch urban fantasy series by the author of the Nikki Ashburne series.

TELLING THE BEES

The amulet was a simple, teardrop-shaped amethyst edged with tiny silver spirals. I wasn't a jewelry maker; I bought the items with which to make the amulets my sister, Willow, and I sold in our Portland shop.

Stone, wood, metal. Simple elements, but part of the earth.

Part of the interwoven magic of the world.

Willow and I don't sell to casual passers-by. Our clientele are true magic users. The shop comprises the front rooms of a purple-and-slate-blue Victorian home, on a side street in the trendy Hawthorne District. Not as easy to find, especially with the wards on it. Sometimes we had to work stronger magic, magic that might be visible or audible or otherwise noticeable to the average person, so we had spells to prevent that.

My workspace was in a second-floor bedroom. The walls were painted a deep, rich blue, like the sky at twilight, but the natural wood trim glowed a dark reddish-brown in the sunlight. Glass-fronted wood cabinets between the windows and doors held tools and supplies. In the center of the room, a round wooden table, close to bistro height, with Celtic knot work etched around the rim, served as my work table

It was a sunny spring day, still cool, but warm enough that I could lift the double-hung windows for a bit of fresh air. The breeze occasionally guttered the flames of the fat white candles ringed on the floor around me, but it wasn't enough to blow them out. The candles helped me focus my magic, allowing me to define and doubly bless my space before I started.

Willow and I are hedgewitches. Willow's talents are with earth, water and plants, so she handles the herbs, potions, tisanes, and other concoctions. Amulets and charms are my purview: air, fire, auras, and protection spells.

Now, gathering up magic from within and around me, I traced invisible symbols on the amethyst, reciting a cantrip as I did. The amethyst shimmered, then glowed as the magic infused it. Amethysts are known for their emotional and spiritual healing properties, and the magic I used was to enhance that, allowing the user to benefit even more from meditations and cleansing rituals. There was a level of protection, too.

Right now, in the world, it felt like everyone needed a little protection from the vast negativity battering at them from all sides.

I finished, closing my eyes and hold my hands, palms up, at waist height for a moment, giving thanks to the universe for my abilities. Then I set the amethyst next to the previous amulet I'd worked on: a flat, polished disk of wood, with a simple triskele etched on it (adding the element of Fire). Into that I'd imbued solidity, groundedness to go along with the already present slow, patient strength of the tree.

I shook out my hands and reached for the next project when a soft knock sounded at the door, followed by Willow's light voice.

"Holly? Sorry to bother you…"

I huffed through my nose. Magic work took preparation, and being interrupted meant I'd have to start over before I could work on anything else.

But I also knew Willow wouldn't interrupt me unless it was important. Really important.

"Come in."

The door opened. Willow's long, light brown hair, streaked with pale green, was piled on her head in a wispy, Gibson-girl style. She wore a floaty, wine-colored skirt edged in crocheted lace, a scoop-neck white shirt, a choker make of crocheted leaves, and a sage-green, open jacket, the light fabric embroidered with burgundy and darker green.

In contrast, my short, darker hair is shot through with dark green, and is spiky like my personality. (Very few people are allowed to say that and live.) I wore skinny jeans, a Prussian blue top, and dangling peacock-feather earrings.

I leaned back, elbows on my work table. "What's going on?"

"Jayden called," Willow said. "He sounded pretty worried."

Jayden. I mouthed the name. It sounded familiar, but I couldn't place it.

"From West Linn," Willow said. When I obviously still wasn't getting it, she added, "The protection bubble?"

Oh, *Jayden*. The annoying kid. The barely trained witch and unlicensed boob who'd botched a protection spell and made my life hell for a day. I let my emotions show on my face. "What's he done now?"

"I'm not sure," Willow said. "He asked for you, and said he really needed help. That it would take too long to explain, and it was urgent."

I held out a hand and pinched my thumb and forefinger together. The candles on the floor went out, leaving behind the sharp scent of trailing smoke.

"Guess I have to go, then."

Our job is to help, not to judge. And yes, I was being my usual cranky self, but it wasn't entirely Jayden's fault that he hadn't been getting the proper training or that his familiar had gone walkabout because he wasn't ready for her.

Mostly his fault, but not entirely.

"I'll go with you," Willow said.

"You sure?"

"I saw how monumentally Jayden can screw up," she said wryly. "I have a feeling this is going to need all of us."

By all of us, she meant the two of us and my familiar, Cam.

For some reason, the story of what a familiar is to a witch got mutated and morphed by the non-magical, like a legendary game of telephone, down through the ages. Now people think familiars are magical animal companions, or animal-shaped spirits, or something along those lines. Sure, Cam could shift into any type of creature he chose, as well as mist, water, a tree, a rock…you name it, Cam can become it.

Because Cam *is* magic. He's one of the fae folk, and that's what witches' familiars are. We can do magic, but the Fae folk can't. They're aligned with the earth, with nature—they're simply pure magic, and we tap that magical essence to help weave and create our spells.

It's a symbiotic relationship, not a master/servant one like the stories of witches and familiars that ordinary people believe. We're partners, equals. Each witch connects with a fae whose magical essence closely dovetails with his or her personal energy, and for lack of a better way to phrase it, we bond for life—although the fae live longer than humans, and can have multiple such relationships throughout their existence. There are a few things that can break the bond, but they're rare. In fact, some familiars stay within a family, although that wasn't the case with Cam.

He wore dark grey trousers and a white button-down shirt. He was tall and slender, but there was a steely core strength to him. His hair was the color of goldenrod, his eyes were stormy blue, and his cheekbones wouldn't cut just glass, but diamonds.

A fae's true name is private, and can change, and is a part of them in a way human names simply aren't. Even though Cam's power was entwined with mine, for him to share his true name with me would be to give up a deep part of himself. Fae didn't do that, and witches didn't ask them to.

Also, their names are impossible for humans to pronounce.

So I called him Cam, short for Camelot, because he has this posh accent that sounds la-di-dah upper-crust British. Because he puts up with me, he's not even offended.

Willow's familiar, Eoin, was missing. She wouldn't talk about it, not even to me.

And Jayden's had decided he needed more training before they could truly form their bond, so she'd ditched him.

So Cam was all we had.

We got in my car, and I cut across Portland to I-205 and headed south.

West Linn was essentially a suburb of Portland, most of it lying along the banks of the Willamette River. The town is known for its falls, its trees, and the massive paper mill that had just closed after more than 120 years of operation. (All of those things were related.) Now, it was also known for being a safe and tony place to live, as McMansions had been built in the hills to take advantage of the great views.

The first thing I noticed when I took Exit 8 off the freeway was that there were no cars on the road. It was the morning of a work day, not quite lunch time, but there should have been *some*. Maybe there was construction somewhere.

Except there were no signs to that effect.

I pulled into the parking lot of the Market of Choice, an Oregon-based grocery chain that wasn't quite as hoity-toity as New Seasons or Whole Foods, but significantly above Safeway and the like.

I'd been here once before, seeking out Jayden. It had been in the middle of an unusually heavy snow season, but even then, there had been shoppers around. The market was behind a row of businesses, from a backyard bird shop to a Vietnamese pho place to a martial arts dojo. A Starbucks, of course. Can't have a business area without a Starbucks. The local library and Post Office were nearby, too. The whole area was surrounded by tall trees, making it feel less strip-mall-y.

There were a few cars in the parking lot and along the street, but no pedestrians.

On a beautiful spring day like this, the area should have been teeming with soccer moms in yoga pants.

We opened our car doors, and as one, froze.

The sound…was wrong.

No cars, obviously, except the faint ones on the freeway bridge crossing the river, less than a mile away. No voices.

Only…humming.

Like a thousand—no, a million voices humming together, a wordless tune. Barely a tune, because each note lasted so long, and eased into the next without a pause or break.

I looked around, then closed my eyes. I couldn't pinpoint a source. I looked at Willow and Cam. They shook their heads.

For some reason, none of us wanted to speak.

The humming wasn't unpleasant. In many ways, it was soothing.

Which did not mean it wasn't entirely weird.

I hate weird.

Jayden had told Willow he'd be inside the market. The glass doors, which had a large sign letting us know we could purchase reusable shopping bags if we'd forgotten ours, parted automatically.

The grocery store was so quiet, I could hear the faint buzz of the fluorescent lights, which normally wouldn't have been obvious over the regular noises of chatting shoppers and check-out people, shelves being stacked, and the cooking going on behind the freshly made food counter along the right.

I could've gone for a slice of pizza, myself, or maybe a wok bowl, but there were more pressing problems.

Like, where were all the people in the middle of the day?

And what was that humming noise outside, which I felt like I could still faintly hear?

Feeding myself came in a reluctant third right now. Which gave me extra motivation to solve questions one and two.

Jayden had been sitting at a black table by the front window, near the espresso bar, to our right behind a cooler of individual bottles of juice and kombucha and snooty water. Because of the silence, I heard the scrape of his chair as he stood.

He was a lanky kid, barely into his twenties, still with a smattering of acne that stood out when he went pale from nervousness. He wore jeans that were torn at the hem, scuffed hiking boots, and a black T-shirt with a faded Led Zeppelin logo.

"What did you do?" I demanded by way of greeting.

He swallowed, his prominent Adam's apple bobbing. "I didn't do anything, I swear! At least...I can't think of anything I might have done that would have caused this."

He was scared of me. This fact brought me great pleasure.

"Caused what?" Willow's voice was gentler than mine. We had Soothing Witch/Cranky Witch thing down pat.

He threw his hand out to indicate the store, or maybe the whole town. "This!"

"The fact that nobody's shopping?" I asked. "You have stock in Market of Choice or something?"

"It's not that," he said. "Everyone's asleep."

"Everyone?" Willow asked, looking alarmed.

"Everyone," he repeated. "The whole town." He bit his lip. "I think we've been cursed."

Curses don't work that way, but this was definitely something bad and wrong.

According to Jayden, the day had started out normally, and then…well, as best he could tell, everyone went home and went back to bed, or curled up beneath their desks, or in the break room here in the store. (There was also a meeting room upstairs here. Some employees had stretched out on the floor and table.) He couldn't wake up his parents, his friends.

It seemed to be limited to West Linn. Across the river, in Oregon City, life was going on as normal.

"And you're not affected," I said. "That makes it look like you did something."

"I swear I didn't," he said. "I've been practicing magic—your friend Burke has been mentoring me—but really low-key and carefully. I didn't do anything yesterday or today."

Unless a deliberate time-release factor was part of a spell, magic was instantaneous.

"We need to find the source of the humming," Willow said. Which was obvious, but I didn't say so. Plus, I could stand here all day blaming Jayden, and that wasn't going to make things better.

My stomach grumbled.

"Let's go, then," I said, waving a hand at the glass doors. "Once more unto the breach."

It didn't take us very long. One of my magical affinities is for animals, so once I sat still and grounded myself and cast out, I found them.

All the many, many, *many* bees.

They were all over West Linn. I mean, *all over*. They were spread out enough that they hadn't been visibly obvious when we'd arrived, and I sensed that the clustered swarms were in the woods and various parks scattered through the small city.

We sat at the openwork metal tables outside the Starbucks. I really wanted to go inside and get a snack, but I refrained.

Plus I'd have to make my drink myself.

Because Cam was pure magic and, essentially, part of nature, I connected with him to communicate with the bees.

I felt his essence dovetail with mine, slide into me—charging me up, so to speak. I took that pure magic and formed it into the tools I needed, and then I reached out to find the nearest queen.

I know enough about bees that you had to go directly to the source.

I frowned. I could sense all the bees—well, not each individual bee as if I were counting them, but I felt their numbers. I found quite a few queens, which also surprised me, because queens didn't usually hang out together. Well, there were a few species that did, but not our happy American honeybees.

I wasn't sure which queen to address. Would I offend them if I spoke to the wrong one? None stood out.

I made a decision, and hoped it was the right one.

Cam gave me a…I'm not sure "word" is a strong enough concept for the almost overwhelming power it carried. It was in the language of the Fae, an ancient language of the earth and air and fire and water that binds the world together.

That word was for the bees. Not a command, but a respectful request.

Without knowing which queen to choose, I had to talk to all of them. At once.

And they responded. All at once. Not just the queens, but *all the damn bees*.

At first it was deafening, but together Cam and I managed to modulate the sound so it was not painful and was easier to understand, and we looped in Willow and Jayden so they could hear, too.

The bees came.

The air cooled as they blocked out the sky, blotted out the sun, before turning every building around us, and the cars and the roads and the parking lots black as they settled. We still couldn't see all of them, I knew; some remained behind, or tucked into the nearby trees.

You can hear usss, the bees said.

"We can," I said. I introduced us, three witches and a familiar.

I got the sense the bees genuflected a tiny bit, but it was hard to say.

"What are you doing?" I asked. "Why have you put the town to sleep?"

It is our ssssong. We are sssso very tired.

"Did the people here do something to you?" I didn't ask if

Jayden was responsible. I really couldn't see how he was, and the bees would point fingers—er, antennae—if it came to that.

All people, the bees said. *Sssso many people. Then our Queen died, and we could not take any more.*

"Any more what?" I could see this was going to take a while. Which made me grumpy. Why couldn't they have at least brought me some honey?

Telling. Telling ussss. The telling of the beesss.

Oh, yeah, like that was a lot of help. I tamped down my annoyance in case they could sense it—I really didn't want this to turn into a 1950s low-budget horror movie—and pondered how to frame my next question when Jayden said, "Oh, I've heard of that!"

Then he added sheepishly, probably because of the expression on my face, "I read a lot."

"Fill us in, please," I said.

"In many cultures, they believed that when something happened in a beekeeper's life, someone had to tell the bees. A marriage, the birth of a child, and especially death. A hive could die out, or stop making honey, or leave because nobody properly told them about their keeper's death."

Sssso many tellingsss. Sssso many ssstoriesss.

Bit by bit, Jayden and I got the bees to explain the real problem.

The bees remembered the stories, and many more—it turned out the "telling" didn't have to be direct, or even only about their own beekeeper. Each hive in turn told their queens, who "carried" the stories with her, and passed them on to future queens. The worker bees collected the stories but could only hold so many; the queens was the only ones who could keep all of them.

The queens, in essence, were the ones with the big hard drives. The workers were more like little thumb drives.

And then there was the matter of the Queen. The Queen of the queens. The biggest memory chip of all.

Who had died.

Now the queens were full, and the workers were full, and they couldn't handle any more stories. They couldn't process any more deaths.

Then Cam dropped the bomb that it went deeper than that, in terms of it being a problem for everyone, not just the bees.

"The bees bridge the natural world with the afterlife," he said. "Without their work, there could be…" He spread his hands. "I'm not even sure how to describe it without it taking days. But it could affect your world, and mine as well, permanently."

"I believe you that it would be really bad," I said. "I think we can move to a solution without knowing all those details, yes?"

Willow and Jayden nodded. The bees hummed in agreement. Good, because I wasn't waiting days for food.

So the bees had put everyone to sleep because they were full of stories and couldn't take any more, even though the stories were banging at them, trying to get in.

Right now, only West Linn had been taken out. There was no telling how fast this would spread, or how far. We could be in deep doo-doo very soon.

We might be battered by negativity from all sides, and in some ways, being lulled to sleep by buzzing bees sounded kind of peaceful, but the world was going to end up a lot worse if we all crashed out.

"How long will it take for you to find a new Queen?" I asked.

Wwe don't knowww.

Damn. "Can you tell the stories to someone else? Something else? In other words, can you store the stories while waiting for a new Queen?"

The bees buzzed amongst themselves, the sound rising and falling. I hoped I hadn't said the wrong thing. They didn't *sound* agitated.

Yesss. We believe that will work.

I pointed. "How about him?"

"Me?" Jayden yelped. "Why me?"

"Because you need training," I said. "You need experience. This is a way for you to learn about people, other people's lives. Not just stuff from books."

"Hey, his book knowledge helped here," Willow pointed out. "But what you're saying makes a lot of sense, actually."

"Sometimes I come up with good ideas," I said.

She shook her head and a ghost of a smile whispered across her lips.

I focused back to the bees. "This man will take your stories, hold them for you," I said. "But first, I need to go to my house and get something for him, to help with the process. Is that acceptable?"

Yesss. And thank you.

I left Cam and Willow in West Linn to hash out any final details with the bees, and drove back north and into Portland. The cars and people were almost startling. There was something to be said for silence, for having only the song of the bees.

When I'd worked on the amethyst amulet earlier this morning, I hadn't been thinking of anyone in particular. Some amulets were commissions, but not this one. This one...when I'd picked up the silver-edged stone, I'd known what it needed to be.

I curled my fingers around it, feeling the magic pulse like a heartbeat.

Like the hum of bees telling their stories.

The amulet would help Jayden process the stories, because the stories were about emotion. The happiest and saddest days of people's lives.

I had a feeling he and the bees were going to be good for each other.

GHOSTED

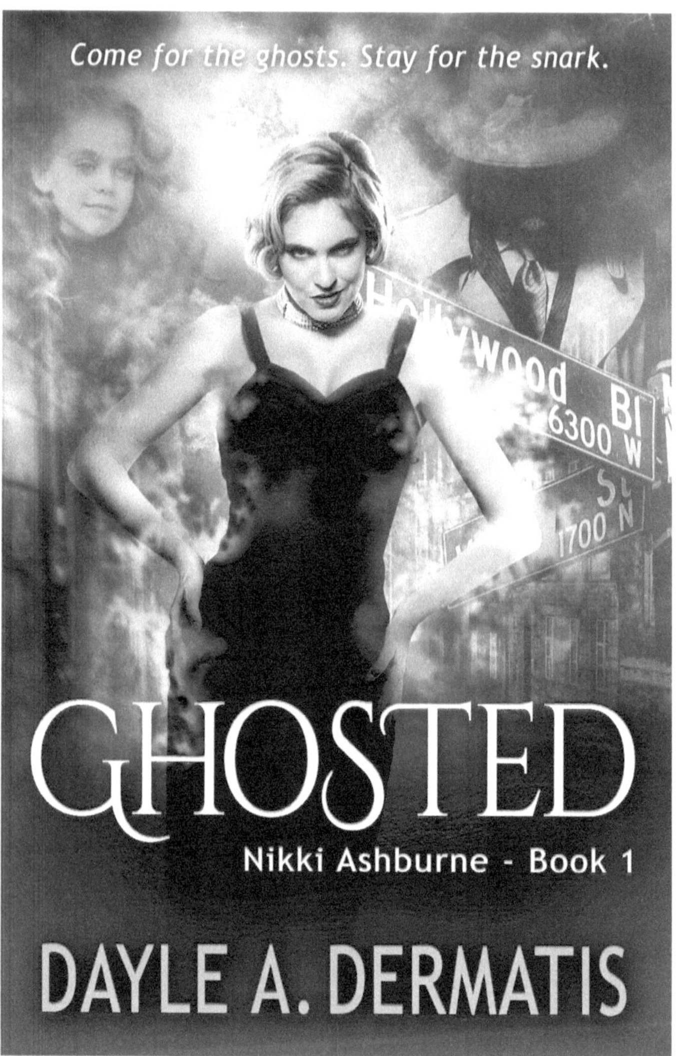

Turn the page for a preview of the first Nikki Ashburne novel, Ghosted!

CHAPTER 1

WHAT WOULD you do if your friends started disappearing, and you didn't know how to stop it?

What if all of those friends were ghosts?

Dude, if you'd asked me that a year ago, I would've told you that was a great pitch line, but my father's the movie producer, not me. I wouldn't have thought you were serious, and if you were, I would've laughed so hard my tequila sunrise would've shot right out of my nose.

Then it happened to me. And nobody's laughing.

You know how in movies, someone will be at a loud party, but they seem to be in a bubble where the sound barely filters through? That was how I felt right now. Around me, people laughed and talked, house music pounded, but it was all…distant.

I moved slowly, making no sudden movements so I didn't break the sphere, which I imagined was thin like a soap bubble, completely invisible.

I still wore the stylish black dress I'd worn earlier today to the funeral; I hadn't wanted to go all the way home to change, although I'd taken off the little hat with the attached veil. No normal twenty-something owns hats like that, but I'd worn it when I played Mourner #5 in one of my father's scream flicks, and I'd kept it, because it was cute. Wardrobe never noticed.

I think my *abuelita*, Grandma Rosa, would have liked it.

I'd left directly from the graveside service to come to the party because I needed the familiar, my comfort zone. But everything felt wrong, different.

I felt different.

Drink in hand, I moved through the crowd, half-seen. It wasn't my first drink of the evening. Gin and tonics, that's what I was drinking this week, because I'd noticed they were what Evan Frohman was drinking, and maybe we could bond over them. After that, I could ease back to drinking things that didn't taste like tree vomit.

We were in a trendy, modern house in the Hollywood Hills—I had no idea who owned it—one that used to be chrome and glass but now, after renovation, was some odd combination of shabby-chic French with Asian accents, and faux-rustic, grey-weathered boards on the walls with painted inspirations like "Breathe" and "Live." On the other hand, the deck, which overlooked the glittering lights of Tinseltown, *was* all glass, to give a dizzying illusion of being suspended in midair.

Wile E. Coyote, I am not. But I could appreciate that the view was spectacular, even as I clutched the nearly invisible edge of the railing with one hand.

My name is Nikki Ashburne. Yes, the daughter of Edward Ashburne, mega-producer, king of the teen sex comedy, sultan of the revival of nighttime soaps. And this (imagine me sweeping my hand over the midnight vista) is my playground.

Yep, I was definitely getting tipsy. Not drunk—not yet—but tonight, unusually, I was steadily working on it.

Even out here, the air clogged with pricy perfume and aftershave. Even out here, I couldn't seem to drag in a full, clean breath of air. Smog wasn't the problem; affluence was.

I raised my glass to that.

Voices invaded my bubble.

"No, she definitely had a nose job. That whole thing about losing baby fat in your cheeks so your nose looks slimmer is bullshit. I know, because I got a nose job for my eighteenth birthday."

"Seriously. Why not just admit it? Almost everybody gets something done for graduation."

"Did you hear about Missy? Another DUI. They're talking about rehab."

"Well, she has *got* to learn to hold her phone lower when she's texting, because then the cops don't see it."

"…sex tape…"

"Who calls them *tapes* anymore? Shit, Becca, you sound like my mother…"

A jumble of voices, but I recognized them all: my peeps. Chris, Eden, Jessica, Samantha, Kayla. They tumbled onto the deck in a flurry of glitter, fashion, and sky-high heels.

"There you are," Eden said, flipping her long blond hair over her shoulder in a motion I'd watched her practice in the mirror. "We've been looking for you *everywhere*."

"Sorry," I said before I could stop myself. "Just not in the mood to tear down someone just because they made a bad choice."

"What is *up* with you tonight?" Jessica asked.

"My grandmother died, remember? Today was her funeral." I felt disconnected as I said it, as if it had happened to someone else. As if I were (freely admitted) a less-than-stellar actress reciting her lines.

Even as I felt disconnected, I knew it was wrong. I was aching—no, it was a sharp pain. Stabbity stabbity in my gut. I downed my drink. I tried to set the highball glass on the balcony, but there was no real balcony, and the glass toppled down to the scrub below.

If anybody noticed, they didn't comment. Or, probably, care. Wasn't their glass.

Although I'd probably be a story later. Pity, I wasn't even all that drunk.

I'm never going to whine about how awful my life is, but the fact is, it's not easy growing up in the public eye. Everything I did was credited to my father paving the way— certainly *I* wasn't pretty enough or talented enough or smart enough. Daddy and I get along great, but he's Edward Ashburne, for crying out loud, which means he's *busy*. And my mother…oh, I did not want to think about my mother right now. I'm not saying she never loved me, but I had been a useful accessory until I got old enough to disagree with her, and then old enough to put her own admitted age in question.

So I'd spent a lot of time with Grandma Rosa, Daddy's mom, over the years. She had her own house on the estate, and even set up a bedroom for me there, and she'd taught me how to make tortillas and read lines with me and told me that I was pretty and talented and most importantly smart enough.

Now she was dead, and I didn't know where to turn. She'd given the best hugs, and I wanted one of them, and I couldn't feel her smooshing me against her ever again.

"Oh, honey, I'm so sorry," Chris said, hugging me. It was a sincere hug as embraces go, but she still made sure not to smudge her makeup.

Chris Yeates, my best friend, my partner in crime, etc. Stunning blond (via a stunning hairdresser) with curves (some of which were financed), star of the reality show *Young and In Love* (although everyone, including Chris, knew that her "in love" was gay, albeit a great friend). She'd been bugging me to do a cameo on the show.

Maybe next week.

Unless they were filming tonight and I'd have a release form shoved in my face on the way out.

They all swarmed me now, each trying to outdo the others with her false sympathy—even, on the periphery, Asia McBride, who was practically a nobody, a wannabe. How had she even been invited here?

A flurry of sympathy: so sorry, oh darling, hugz, sweetie, what can we do.

"Thanks," I said, blinking back tears. "The funeral was hard..."

I realized my mistake as they went blank. They were sympathetic, but not to the point that I was allowed to bring down the party atmosphere. They'd done their duty—wasn't that enough? Why was I still going on about it?

My grandmother was dead, and all my friends needed everything to be normal.

"Thanks," I repeated, flashing the winning smile I'd learned when my mother entered me in those awful pageants. I mimed shaking an empty glass, since mine had flung itself to its doom. "Let me get a refill, and then you can tell me all about Missy—did she do a duck face for the mug shot again?"

My bubble and I drifted back through the house, through the cigarette and pot smoke, the throb of bass, past Evan who was doing one-armed pushups, surrounded by a throng of admirers.

This time, I asked for a double shot of tequila, which the

bartender provided because bartenders at these types of parties are paid not to ask questions or spill to the press afterwards.

I downed it in three gulps, which burned like hell but made me feel badass for three-tenths of a second. I blinked rapidly to avoid messing up my mascara.

I got another G&T, because I needed something in my hand. I started back for the balcony, but I just didn't have the energy to put on the face they wanted to see.

Evan was now standing on a coffee table for some reason. I saluted him with my drink, and he winked.

I didn't have the energy to do more than flash a smile, but when I felt better…

The pain rolled through me, fresh as a thousand paper cuts splashed with lime juice and salt. How could I ever feel better? How could that be *possible*?

That's when I saw them. No, not ghosts—that would come later. Although these, and this choice I was about to make, would forever haunt me.

The pretty crystal bowl of pills, pink and blue and yellow like cheap candy from a piñata. Candy that offered way more than a sugar rush.

I'd never done drugs. Never really considered it; despite tonight's chase-the-pain-away efforts, I wasn't even that much of a drinker beyond a few social glasses.

My bubble seemed to increase in strength; the world, the party, the people all seemed more distant. I looked around. No one was watching me—but that's not why I looked. I wasn't feeling guilty, and I was certainly far from the first person here to indulge. In very great hindsight, I think I was looking for someone to break the bubble, to connect with me. But I was alone. Hurting and alone.

And this seemed like the only way to numb the pain. Couldn't make it worse, right?

I have no idea what I chose. I just sort of grabbed two, slid them down my throat with a sip of fizzy pine sap.

I went back out on the deck, already feeling numb from the tequila, and rejoined my friends, smiling and dropping random comments when I was expected to.

And then I started to feel awful. Not just alcohol-spinning awful—I knew this was worse. I knew I'd fucked up, badly, and the horror that comes with that knowledge washed through me. Blackness swarmed at the edge of my sight, and for the second time that night, I dropped my drink. Someone must've realized what was going on because I heard shouts about calling 911 and then everyone was swarming again and I was heading for lights-out.

Well, shit.

Kids, don't try this at home.

There's a lot I don't remember. I have no memory of the ambulance ride, which sucks because I would've liked to have experienced the siren. Is it like on TV? Maybe I'll never know.

I don't remember the ER, which is probably a good thing. Well, I have a vague sense that there was some shouting, and sharp smells, and I'm guessing they stuck tubes down my throat, but who wants to remember that?

This is what I remember: somebody pinching my arm, and then waking up in a room that would have been quiet except for some infernal machine making a pinging noise and some other machine humming.

It was worse than a hangover. My tongue felt fuzzy and my mouth was coated with some thick goo that tasted like battery acid. I reached for water and that made my arm pinch more, so I reluctantly opened my eyes.

I did not know that acoustic tile ceiling.

Everything came into focus slowly, including my brain. I took in the IV—the source of the pinching—the whiteboard on the wall across from the foot of my bed with the date and time and "your nurse's name is Jeannie"; the annoying puffs of air in my nose that turned out to be an oxygen feed; the streaking sunbeams that made me squint.

I felt kinda floaty, and yet my head hurt, which seemed unfair.

I'd learn later that I had a *very* nice private room in a wing of the hospital most people don't even know about. The rich-and-famous wing. The spare-no-expenses wing.

Even though my bed was propped up a bit, it took me several tries to struggle into something resembling a seated position. There was a pitcher of water and a Styrofoam cup and a straw on a rolling tray table, but they were way beyond my abilities to reach, much less hold on to.

"Hello?" Well, I *tried* to say it. I mostly kind of croaked through my Death Valley of a mouth.

The money-has-no-object wing doesn't include a nurse who can't take potty breaks, apparently.

I was looking around for some sort of call button—slowly, because if I turned my head too fast, the room went all spinny, but in a slow-motion kind of way that still made me want to hurl—when I realized there was, in fact, someone in the room with me.

Someone who hadn't been there a moment ago, and who hadn't come in the door.

My *abuelita*, my beloved grandmother—the grandmother whose funeral I had recently attended (How long ago was that? How long had I been here?)—was sitting on the bed.

It was the drugs. Had to be. Making me hallucinate.

She was the same fireplug of a woman I'd seen buried,

wearing the royal blue suit she'd had on when she died, with the gold peacock brooch with precious gems in the tail that she'd loved so much—the first major purchase my father had made after his first movie that made it big—pinned on the lapel. (My mother had thrown a royal fit when she'd learned Grandma wanted to be buried with it. I'm surprised she hadn't figured out a way to sneak into the funeral home and replace it with a fake. As if my mother's jewelry wasn't all a gazillion times more expensive.)

It was my grandmother, all right, her skin tanned and wrinkled, her hair as black as the last day she'd dyed it, her dark eyes flashing like they did when she beat me at Rummikub *again*.

Only that wasn't teasing, affectionate triumph in her gaze.

No, her expression was dead clear (pardon the pun): she was *royally pissed off*.

I tried to say something, but the lack of saliva tripped me up again.

It probably wouldn't've helped.

Because my grandmother said, "Nikki Elizabeth Ashburne, how could you be so *stupid?*"

Her palm cracked against my cheek. The sting of it slapped through my prescription-drug floatiness, and I sucked in my breath.

"Don't you *ever* do something like that again!" Grandma Rosa hissed, and then she was gone.

Just, *poof*, gone.

I might've been able to explain it away as a hallucination if my mother hadn't walked in right then, seen the handprint on my face, and raised holy hell. Shrieking was involved. Lawsuits were threatened. Mayhem ensued.

In the quiet center of the vortex, finally sipping some

blessed cool water through a bendy straw, I accepted the truth. My life was no longer what it had been.

I could see ghosts.

ABOUT THE AUTHOR

Dayle A. Dermatis is the author or coauthor of many novels (including snarky urban fantasies *Ghosted* and the forthcoming *Shaded* and *Spectered*) and more than a hundred short stories in multiple genres, appearing in such venues as *Fiction River*, *Alfred Hitchcock's Mystery Magazine*, and DAW Books.

Called the mastermind behind the *Uncollected Anthology* project, she also guest edits anthologies for *Fiction River*, and her own short fiction has been lauded in many year's best anthologies in erotica, mystery, and horror.

She lives in a book- and cat-filled historic English-style cottage in the wild greenscapes of the Pacific Northwest. In her spare time she follows Styx around the country and travels the world, which inspires her writing.

To find out where she's wandered off to (and to get free fiction!), check out DayleDermatis.com and sign up for her newsletter or support her on Patreon.

I value honest feedback, and would love to hear your opinion in a review, if you're so inclined, on your favorite book retailer's site.

For more information:
www.dayledermatis.com

BE THE FIRST TO KNOW!

Sign up for Dayle A. Dermatis's newsletter for *free* fiction, plus the latest news, releases, and more.

Sign up at DayleDermatis.com.

For more in-depth conversations and special sneak peeks, you can also support her continued work by joining her community of supporters at Dayle's Patreon.

Patreon.com/Dayle